H. M. (Herman Milton) Bien

Oriental Legends

And other Poems

H. M. (Herman Milton) Bien

Oriental Legends
And other Poems

ISBN/EAN: 9783744764551

Printed in Europe, USA, Canada, Australia, Japan

Cover: Foto ©Andreas Hilbeck / pixelio.de

More available books at **www.hansebooks.com**

ORIENTAL ✠

✠ LEGENDS

AND

OTHER POEMS.

OM MANI·PADME HUM.·-BUDDHA

BY

RABBI H. M. BIEN.

NEW YORK:
BROWN & DERBY, PUBLISHERS.
1883.

ERRATA.

In consequence of the great distance from the author to the place of publication, the following errors remained uncorrected :

Page 38, line 9 read : "Chasidim" instead of "the Chasidim."

" 38, " 19 " "That parents" instead of "And parents."

" 46, " 16 " "and there" instead of "and then."

" 49, " 16 " "concocted rash" instead of "concocted"

" 57, " 12 " "concocted rash" instead of "concocted."

" 52, " 9 " "curst" instead of "cursed."

" 54, " 7 " "curst" instead of "cursed."

" 78, " 7 " "was bereft a mother" instead of "mourns her lost—a mother."

" 78 " 15 " "a yearning mother" instead of "bereft a mother."

" 78 " 16 " "moans" instead of "mourns."

" 79 " 7 " "Rest in peace! all" instead of "Reste in pace."

" 125 " 14 add dash after "Ghetto."

" 132 " 15 read "Till its abode, if" instead of "Until its abode."

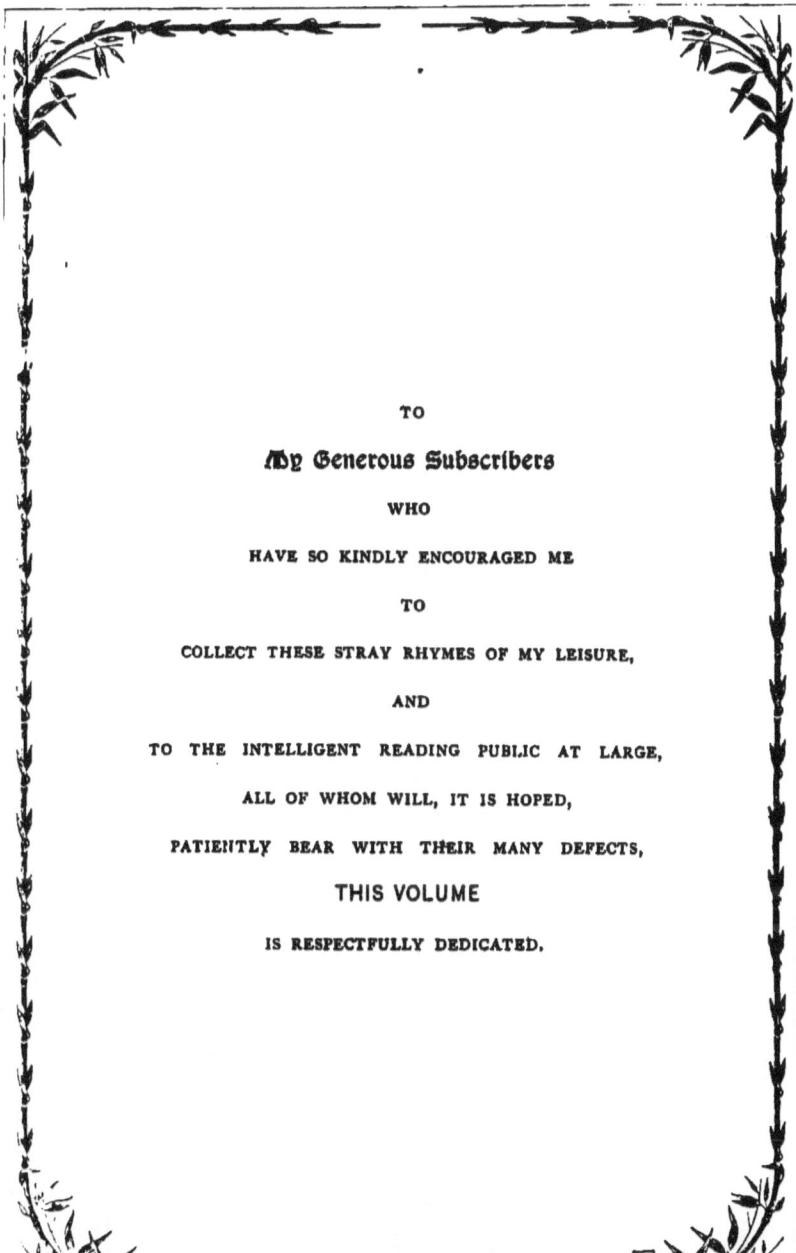

TO

My Generous Subscribers

WHO

HAVE SO KINDLY ENCOURAGED ME

TO

COLLECT THESE STRAY RHYMES OF MY LEISURE,

AND

TO THE INTELLIGENT READING PUBLIC AT LARGE,

ALL OF WHOM WILL, IT IS HOPED,

PATIENTLY BEAR WITH THEIR MANY DEFECTS,

THIS VOLUME

IS RESPECTFULLY DEDICATED.

CONTENTS.

OTHER POEMS.

EPITOMA JUDAICA.

ORIENTAL LEGENDS.

I have read your various "Oriental Legends" with great interest and pleasure.—H. W. LONGFELLOW.

PROEM.

THIS blank sheet of writing-paper
    At which I now careless glance,
  Half in dream and half in trance,
Serves, perhaps, as toy or taper,
    At the will of fate or chance.
In the cause of God or devil
It may work for good or evil—
    Truth proclaim or ignorance.

Or may be a merchant failing,
    Stays his ruin yet awhile
  With this scrap and by his guile.
Nay, some prisoner at the railing
    Trusting Mercy's hopeful smile,
Feels his heart sink, deathly smitten,
When the jury's verdict, written,
    By this paper, goes on file.

Or perchance some bashful lover,
    With a trembling or a frown,
  Tries to write his passion down;
Or the leaf becomes a cover

For some trick of rogue or clown.
It has power to bind and sever,
To enslave or free forever,
Sink or raise a realm or crown.

Who, who dare claim the decision
Its true purport or its way
To predict, or guess, or say?
Such, ha, ha! is human vision!
Speculate as e'er we may,
It ends most like this in vapor;
Served already has the paper
For a Minstrel's roundelay.

Oriental Legends.

THE BIRTH OF THE HEART.

HAVE ever you heard the tradition of old,
Amongst the Orientals often told,
How that beautiful part,
The human heart—
Heaven's own image and counterpart,
Angelic essence, spirit and mould—
Was wrought at the final hour of creation,
Idea sublime, God's best inspiration?

The story is certainly good to repeat;
And thus it doth run: All fair and complete,
The universe stood,
In the attitude
Of youth and perfection, grand and good.
The Sabbath approached. At the Maker's feet,

In clay, stood, the form of Adam created;
The breath of life he only awaited.

The angels to whom had been assigned
The forming of first of humankind,
    With pride and zest
    Had done their best
To make him superior to all the rest—
Perfection, use, and beauty combined.
Alas! the most vital part, they lamented,
Had been forgotten; too late they repented.

The heart they omitted! In trouble and shame
Bowed down before the Almighty, they came.
    "How shall we atone
    For duty undone?"
Then spake the Lord: "Peace, every one!
Go gather quick, in My holy name,
What fragments are left from My six days'
    labor."
Each joyfully hastened away with his neighbor.

And presently every one returns
In hope that speed forgiveness earns.
    And such a string
    Of scraps they bring,

Incongruous and everything.
It seems they gathered from endless concerns
Abundance of stern and grotesque material,
Solids and fluids, gross and aerial.

One brought of lion's pomposity,
Another of tiger's ferocity;
  With jackal's greed,
  And antelope's speed,
Courage and pride of the wilderness' steed;
The fox's guile, the wild goat's glee,
The serpent's cunning, the lamb's mild fea-
  tures—
The virtue and vice of all living creatures.

The song of the birds, the howl of the wolf;
The ripple of fountains, the roar of the gulf;
  The flowers' perfume;
  The smell of the tomb;
The light of the sun and dark night's gloom;
With acid muriatic and nitric and sulph.,
Heat of the flame and glaciers frozen—
Of life and death some each had chosen.

The Lord in mercy and kindness smiled
When He saw what was brought to His hu-
   · man child;

And He added Love—
Bright, shining dove!—
Strengthened by Hope for here and Above,
And covered the whole with Charity mild;
Then breathed in man's nostrils the life he
awaited.
And Sabbath had come! The World was
created!

Thus runs in tradition the legend of old,
Amongst the Orientals often told:
How that beautiful part,
The human heart—
Heaven's own image and counterpart;
Its angel essence and spirit and mould,
Idea sublime, God's best inspiration—
Was wrought at the final hour of creation.

THE CREATION OF MAN.

"And Elohim said, Let us make man in our own image and
likeness."—GENESIS i. 26.

FROM out the quaint Agadah* of old
Talmudic fame
This mystical tradition of man's creation
came :
In six days were completely the earth and
heaven made,
With all their hosts—"And very good they
are ! " the Lord hath said.
        Entire the work is done,
        Except the final one—
That one in whom without a doubt it shall
be demonstrated :
He is the crown and masterpiece of every-
thing created.

Then each celestial legion, the angels far and
, near,
Immediately were summoned for council to
appear.

* The legendary part of the Talmud.

Harmonious ring hosannas in welling, swell-
    ing tone,
Till music fills the endless sphere, when God
    spake from His throne:
      " My will, My scope and plan,
      It fits: let Us make man!
To rule the world and all thereof 'tis My ma-
    ture reflection;
But whosoever choose may urge now any fair
    objection."

Forthwith entreated Justice, whose words
    like prayer seem:
" Thy wisdom, Heavenly Father, in all things
    is supreme!
But man called to existence will right defy,
    and oh!
With cruelty, wrong, and lawlessness, with
    anguish, tears, and woe,
      The guiltless earth he'll fill;
      Therefore abide Thy will!
Ah! keep unstained this perfect world, whose
    beauties are unnumbered;
Create him not, nor mar nor spoil this globe
    by man encumbered."

The angel Truth next uttered this earnest,
    fervent plea :
" We all submit devoutly to Thy divine decree.
O Father! wherefore wilt Thou not from this
    work abstain ?
For man, when once created, will never more
    refrain,
        With calumny and lie,
        Thy kingdom to defy ;
Veracity from earth will part, and happiness
    will vanish.
Create him not! Thus falsehood Thou wilt
    from creation banish ! "

Now Freedom quick stepped forward and
    pleaded piteously :
" If Thou, O God! must fashion this man, let
    me first die ;
For in his wake are coming destructive, crush-
    ing trains—
Oppression, tyranny, and slaves with shackles,
    bonds, and chains.
        His advent sure will stay
        On earth Thy glorious sway."

All Heaven seemed moved at these sad words,
    tearful exclaimed and kneeling:
"Create him not! leave man undone!"—thus
    Liberty's appealing.

There was a hush of silence, as from the fore-
    most band
A trio of seraphim came forward, hand in
    hand;
Like symphonies resounded sweet their united
    prayer:
"Create, O Lord! create Thou man; entrust
    him to our care.
        Untired and firm, though mild,
        We'll ever lead Thy child
From sin and error of the earth, high to sal-
    vation's region.
Create him, Lord!" thus loud implore Love,
    Faith, and Hope—Religion.

From dust of earth Elohim formed man, to end
    this strife.
And then into his nostrils God breathed the
    breath of life.

In his own image and likeness created Adam
    He :
And blessed him with dominion o'er the land
    and o'er the sea ;
        Endowed him most sublime,
        To reach his goal betime,
Ordaining that humanity in holy troth be
    plighted
To Justice, Truth, to Freedom, Love, to Faith
    and Hope united.

THE CREATION OF WOMAN.

THUS runs the parable the rabbins have
    related
How in the world's beginning woman was
    created :
    " It is not good that man should be alone,"
The Lord said, as He summoned to His
    throne
The hosts of Heaven. " Adam must be mated !
    God and two loving hearts alone shall be
    but One."

And then was brought before the angels with-
out number
Adam, the first of man, in deep and death like
slumber.
　To every human part was speech supplied,
　For each to state which one should make
　the bride.
They must, however, not God's plan encumber,
　Her truly to become his helpmate, friend,
　and guide.

Now Heaven was filled with loud and eloquent
recitals
Of heart and brains, of trunk and all the limbs
and vitals.
　Each one most fervent urged his special
　cause,
　As litigants obscure or unmade laws.
Such stretched importance, claims, unheard-of
titles!
　One would have thought the world with-
　out them came to pause.

At last, when vanity and self-praise long had
spoken,
A rib stood bashful forth and plead: "I'm
but a token

Of modest merit, trying by the grace
Of Thee, my Maker, to fill out my place ;
I know that I must bend, or will be broken ;
  Submission is my claim, unselfishness my
  case."

" Thou art the chosen!" spake the Lord, " and
  here I shower
Upon thee all man's highest concentrated
  power."
One touch of His creative hand did weave
Such beauty, grace, such love, strength to
  believe,
Such amiability, a woman's dower,
  That all celestials sang hosanna—born was
  Eve.

Then Adam woke, and there beheld with dazed
  sensation,
His loving, longing, fervent, erst imagina-
  tion ;
The being comely, modest, pure, and fresh,
Into his arms entwines as in a mesh.
" Thou mother of all future generations,
  Bone art thou of my bone," he cries, " flesh
  of my flesh !"

Thus runs the parable the rabbins have re-
lated,
How in the world's beginning woman was
created.
And God blessed marriage, and this law
He gives:
That man his father and his mother leaves;
And when two hearts in love are truly mated,
They One become, as each unto the other
cleaves.

PARADISE LOST AND REGAINED.

MOST tender of stories the East has re-
tained,
How Eden was lost once and fully regained.
Inscribed in their lore-books, they always in
dite it
The song of "Sweet Home!" and they often
recite it.

For primal transgression were banished precise,
The first of our parents from out paradise.
An angel came quickly, expelling the mortals,
His sword, with its flaming sweeps, guarding
the portals.

Forlorn and bewildered, and all in despair,
Stood, weeping and moaning, the desolate pair.
Now Adam exclaimed loud: "From Eden
    drove hither,
Where shall we find comfort? go whither—
    oh! whither?"

And Eve on his bosom did pitiful cry:
"Alas! disobedient and sinful was I."
As thus they lamented, the angel felt sorry
To see them thus troubled, to hear them thus
    worry;

And slowing the swing of his glittering blade,
In mildest of accents he unto them said:
"Bewail your apparent misfortune no longer;
Submission and patience make all of us stronger.

"Resign ye the loss—by God it was planned.
Now make you an Eden yourself! Understand,
No matter how poor and no matter how
    wealthy;
No matter how suffering, ill, or how healthy;

"No matter the distance, condition, or time,
And spite of all hardships of seasons or clime;

No matter what Providence fates for to-morrow,
Come tears or come smiles, come joy or come
sorrow;

"Wherever you wander and whither you roam,
Your Eden you'll find where you build up your
home—
A home filled with quiet, with peace, and con-
tentment,
Without the arch-tempter, the serpent Resent-
ment;

"A home which is filled with the purest of love,
With best gift of Eden—the trust in Above."
So spoke the kind cherub! They listened as-
tonished;
In heart and in soul they felt strong, thus ad-
monished.

Thus regained for man is, by angel's advice,
The Home! May God bless it—the lost Paradise!
From th' East to the West, by all nations des-
canted,
The song of "Sweet Home" will forever be
chanted.

THE FIRST-BLOWN ROSE.

I.

I T is not every one who knows
How erst bloomed forth the first blown
Rose,
As sung in grove and told in tent,
A legend of the Orient;
Still cherished as in by-gone times.
Thus run the rhythm and the rhymes:
Where the desert meets the mountain rising
from the burning sands,
Far away from palm and lotus, crippled, dwarfed,
a thorn-bush stands.
Never had a flower opened from beneath its
twigs or leaves;
Covered with the dust of ages, droopingly it
sways and grieves.
From afar and from anear
It must, humbled, mutely hear
Taunt and spite, and sore reproaches of luxu-
riant oasis;
From the haughty Leb'non cedars to the tini-
est valley daisies.

3

II.

'Tis even-tide. The Occident glows.
Now big dew-tears the foliage throws
On parchèd roots which claw the rocks,
When far away the bleat of flocks
Wakes faint the echoes from the height,
From whence a man appears in sight.
Tenderly the shepherd carries on his breast a
· little lamb
Which had strayed and would have perished,
separated from its dam,
Had not lovingly its guardian, Moses, safely
borne it hence.
Then it was resolved in Heaven, by decree of
Providence:
Who such tender mercy shows
To dumb creatures' need and woes,
Sure is fit for greater labor; his shall be the
high commission,
That he lead, from Egypt's bondage, Isr'el free
to noblest mission.

III.

As down the steep declivity
The Hebrew prophet comes, lo! see,

At Horeb's base, the strangest fire!
It burns and burns, nor does expire;
Nor does consume a single rush;
Nor smoke exhales the flaming brush!
Exodus, the whole third chapter, this event in
     Holy Writ,
Full of highest inspiration, hath recorded,
     grandly fit:
Miracles wrought here at nightfall, stay of
     some of Nature's laws,
These sublime events foreshadowed Free-
     dom's origin and cause.
First-blown Rose, traditions say,
Graced the bush at dawn of day;
And its glorious seed grew ever, envy of all
     vegetation.
Desert-born, it blooms, an emblem: Heaven's
     true love for God's own nation.

SOLOMON'S JUDGMENT.

THE holy tabernacle, the people's outer
    court,
Is thronged, for all Jerus'lem is wild with
    strange report.
Yet soon the stirred commotion subsides and
    all bend low—
King Solomon is coming in royal pomp and
    show.

The silver horns' alarum proclaim in clarion
    tone :
His majesty for judgment ascends his father's
    throne.
No precedent had ever the case he is to hear ;
Before the high tribunal two women do ap-
    pear.

One brings in court an infant—a lovely, living
    child,
Sublimely personating all that is pure and
    mild.   ...

The other, too, she carries a boy, but he is
  dead—
Like envy and disappointment is drooping low
  her head.

"My Lord, oh! give me judgment," she with
  the corpse exclaims;
"This wicked woman weeping, her sex and
  nation shames.
One dwelling since Passover we occupied
  alone,
And both became there mothers ere yet a
  month was gone.

"Imagine, then, my terror, at break of day
  this morn,
Awaking from my slumbers I'd nurse the
  newly-born;
I find this choked, dead bastard right lying
  on my arm—
Exchanged she had the infants: her own did
  meet with harm!"

Thus hoarse, yet loud, she clamors, in attitude
  to wrest
The suckling who is closely hugged to the
  other's breast.

But the accused sobs broken: "O king! do
    hear me plead!
This is my own, believe me—my flesh and
    blood indeed."

"The little one—behold him! How sweetly—
    see, he smiled!
Oh! surely thou wilt never bereave me of
    my child?"
"Thy child! No, mine!" alternate vociferous
    they repeat.
But now the king bids, "Silence!" while ris-
    ing from his seat.

A bodyguard he summons: "Both children
    take, and hew
Them firmly with thy broadsword, for Justice
    sake, in two;
And give to each her portion—the living one
    slay first."
"So mote it be!" cries boldly the one who
    spoke out erst.

According to the mandate, the soldier, though
    he shakes,
His weapon raised already, the weeping infant
    takes.

"Have mercy!" cries the other; "give her
    the live child—stay!"
"No," quoth the first, "divide them; let Jus-
    tice have her sway."

"Hold, hold!" commands the sovereign. He
    gladly was obeyed;
And from the throne descending, to her who
    kneels he said,
While in his arms, moved deeply, the babe to
    her he bore:
"Thou truly art his mother! I doubt thy
    claim no more.

"Here, take thy son!" The people shout till
    the air did ring:
"Hail! God hath given wisdom to Solomon,
    our king!
Thrice hail! He hath established the law di-
    vine Above:
It shall be known for ever a mother's heart
    and love!"

KING AND PROPHET.

"Come now and let us reason together, saith the Lord: Though your
sins be as scarlet, they shall become as white as snow; though they be red
like crimson, they shall be as wool."—Isaiah i, 18.

I.

YON in his blood lies welt'ring a noble
warrior slain,
Betrayed by royal sycophants, a hero in their
craven train ;
Unto his wife the sovereign adulterous love
has nursed,
Therefore Uriah needs must die, but David
lives disgraced and cursed.

II.

The misled woman sobs, all fears,
Uncomforted, in floods of tears :
" I loved him, heart and soul, alone ;
My grief will not my guilt atone."

Since David in her arms reposed
Sleep never has his eyelids closed ;
A bloody shadow of affright,
A spectre haunts him day and night.

III.

Crowned and sceptred sate
In the temple's gate
David as judge—in Hebrew, "Shofet."
He and the people behold,
In dignity of old,
Nathan, the aged seer and prophet.

Cries: "Whom wrongs aggrieve
Justice must receive,
King!—for this are kings appointed.
List, then, to my case,
Heartless, vile, and base,
And redress it, Lord's anointed!

IV.

"Sire, there lives within thy realms
· One whom fortune ever favored,
But, though wealth him overwhelms,
Greedy, he has never wavered
To envy his poor neighbor's share—
An only lamb, his love and care.

4

"Guests came to the miser; hence,
　　Spite remonstrance, spite of tear,
He forthwith, on some pretence,
　　All that to the poor is dear
Kills; the cherished pet it died.
Sire, thy judgment I abide."

Wild with indignation cries
　　David, rising: "Here I swear
The villain who hath done this dies;
　　Let his goods the pauper share!"
"King! thou art that man!" the seer
Answers. "Be accursed for e'er!"

V.

Ah! Death spares not youth and never minds
　　age;
　　A beggar he smote on the street, and since
He gathered a fool and garnered a sage,
　　And from David's palace he snatched him
　　a prince.

The stricken parents stand by the corse,
　　Lamenting and weeping in anguish and fear;
Royalty harrowed with deepest remorse,
　　His eyes overflowing with tear upon tear.

But all at once a sudden impulse
   Comes o'er the father; he kneels by his
     dead.
The heart which revolted, his feverish pulse,
   Grow quiet, and upward his gaze is led.

Resigned, he folds his hands and prays:
   "Heavenly Father, deign list to my word:
Sinner I am, and just are Thy ways,
   Yet deal with me merciful, Lord, O my
     Lord!"

The prophet, behold! he stands by his side
   And bids him arise, for God commands.
Curses are powerless when we confide
   In Providence; trustful raise hearts and
     hands.

Exalted the king and consoled he became,
   Exclaiming these words immortally graced;
"The Lord hath given and taken; the name
   Of the Lord forever and ever be praised!"

JOCHANNAN BEN SAKKAI.

A HISTORICAL SKETCH.

I.

THAT was the strangest fun'ral which
    ever was beholden
Among the Hebrew people of modern times
    or olden.
No crowd of mourners follow, nor music's
    muffled strain.
Two students lift the coffin, one Rabbi heads
    the train.
    From the city of disaster
    They'll carry out the master.
Ben Sakkai—woe! the priest is dead! The
    sad report goes quickly out,
'Midst siege beyond, turmoil within, and gen'ral
    broil and crazy bout.
Young Joshua and El'asar bear the pall with all
    that's mortal;
Batiach old, the comrade true, leads to the for-
    tress portal.

II.

Up to the gate portcullised the burden slow
    is carried;
But there the sent'nel halts them, who rather
    not had tarried.
" My orders are that nothing must pass be-
    yond the wall,
Except I be permitted to first inspect it all."
      The leader, disappointed,
      Exclaims: " The Lord's anointed,
When dead, who dares defile by touch, he is
    accursed! Come, let us go."
" Move on! move quick!" rejoins the guard;
    " my nose tells all I need to know."
Slow they proceed till soon is reached the
    gate; then, like forsaken,
They hurry to the Roman camp, where they
    are captives taken.

III.

Vespasian here, the gen'ral, for months has
    grimly striven
To crush the hated Hebrews, to fierce sedi-
    tion given,

With battering-rams and siege-trains bombard-
ing day and night
Strong-fortified Jerus'lem, who resolute makes
fight.

    But inside, mad contention,
    Fanatical dissension;
The sects and clans rage blind and tear the
suffering people all apiece.
The Chasidim * and the Sadducee, the Naza-
rene and Pharisee—
Each one strives for the mastery, to bring the
others under;
While outside steadily the foes against the
city thunder.

IV.

In vain appeal the starving for bread or for
surrender;
Despair and hunger vainly implore in tones
most tender;
And parents their own children in frenzy slay
and eat,
And babes suck on dead mothers, their nour-
ishment to meet.

* Hebrew name of the Essenes; literally the Pious.

Forsooth! as in all ages,
Prophetical the sages
Proclaim such folly's certain end, and cry
    aloud : "For God's sake stay
This fratricidal, murd'rous feud, nor let your
    passions reign or sway ;
Appease at once the conqueror, outside, while
    yet in season."
But who has ever known wild mobs like these
    to value reason?

v.

When baffled in all efforts to have his warning
    heeded,
To squelch rebellion and restore the union
    sadly needed ;
When foiled in every measure to stay the
    wrath to come
By flattering the enemy, their mighty foe of
    Rome,
      At last the high-priest wily
      A way devises slyly
By which he'll save himself and people, al-
    though he sees the horror all,
Sees Isr'el's nationality, her glory, and her
    Temple fall.

'Tis patent in her hare-brained strifes, 'tis by
    her seers written :
" So shall their mission be fulfilled ! so be her
    folly smitten ! "

VI.

Approved in sacred council, his death is soon
    reported ;
He's laid into a coffin and out of town es-
    corted.
And so that the deception in detail be com-
    plete,
He suffers that beside him is placed some
    putrid meat.
        Most killed by suffocation,
        Yet soon his restoration
In their besieger's camp is slow but fully by
    kind hands attained,
While officers and soldiers laugh, nor silent
    would be or restrained. '
Forthwith the resurrected corpse into the
    gen'ral's presence
Is led to make his errand known, its meaning
    and its essence.

VII.

"Know, chieftain! paper arrows were shot
    thee from our city
My prophecy conveying — remember it, I
    prithee!
Our God hath pleased to forestall through me
    that thou shalt reign
The world as Latin emperor; now let me not
    in vain
        Beseech thee for this favor."
        Thus plead, all in a quaver,
The tottering, white-haired, aged priest: "Give
    us permission now to go
Unto the town of Jabne, where we'll hide away
    from shame and woe
Thou bringest on our people sure.   Have
    mercy, Cæsar—ora!
Let me establish there a school to teach our
    holy Torah."

VIII.

The Roman mused a minute ere, deeply moved,
    addressing
The captives; he salutes them: "Give, Rabbins,
    me your blessing;

5

Your modest wish is granted; now go ye hence
    in peace,
And that your work may prosper, my prayer
    shall never cease."   ·
        Soon after they departed :
        The Talmud-school was started,
It rose and flourished grandly, too, as hist'ry
    does explicit tell,
A bulwark to their people, who had seen how
    shrine and city fell.
The first of the " Ta-na-im " * here have taught
    what was most needed,
A codex for all Isr'el, which has never been
    exceeded.

IX.

Empires have risen and fallen; cities were built
    and destroyed;
Nations have flourished and withered; war and
    peace were employed,
Generation after generation, to shape and form
    incessant
The status of society, the future, past, and
    present.

---

* The experts and transmitters of the oral law at the time of the second
destruction of the Temple are called the " Tanaim."

But nothing more conclusive
In all proved so conducive
For e'er to lead the human race unto its final,
   noble goal,
To prop up tolerance and truth and elevate
   the human soul,
Than law, philosophy, and rules, as taught
   here and expounded,
The heirlooms from the "Jabne" school by
   this Ben Sakkai founded.

THE BEST AND THE WORST.

" SEARCH the bazaar," said the sheik to
   the slave,
   "And get me the Best which the markets
      provide."
The slave salamed lowly, the slave answered
   grave:
   "Thy will shall be done; in my judgment
      abide,"
And soon, on returning, said: "Rightly or
   wrong,
I bring here the Best of the market—a tongue."

"Search the bazaar," said the sheik to the
    slave,
  "And get me the Worst which the markets
    provide."
The slave salamed lowly, the slave answered
    grave :
  " Thy will shall be done ; in my judgment
    abide,"
And soon, on returning, said : " Rightly or
    wrong,
I bring here the Worst of the market—a
    tongue ! "

" Explain what thou meanest ! " cried the sheik
    to the slave.
  " I'll give thee thy freedom if well thou
    decide."
The slave salamed lowly, the slave answered
    grave :
  " Thy will must be done; my judgment
    abide.
Now listen and say if I'm right or if
    wrong :
The Best and the Worst in the world is the
    tongue.

" The tongue to a freedman quick changes a
 slave ;
 The tongue enslaves quickly the free,
  though he died ;
The tongue rules the world, from cradle to
 grave ;
 The tongue sways the khedive and beggar beside."
" Thy tongue made thee free! Thou argued
 it strong,"
Laughed the sheik. " The Best and the Worst
 is the tongue ! "

DOG, HORSE, AND HOG.

AN EASTERN FABLE.

GOOD neighbors and friends were a horse
and a dog.
Not far from them wallowed a fattening hog.
The first two were regularly fed thrice a day,
While the sow is allowed to munch all that
she may.
Said the cur to the horse : " It seems not to
me fair
That the swine should eat more than belongs
to its share."

The stallion replied : " Wait a little, my friend ;
Thou'lt see we fare best by our stint in the
end."
The piggy, well fattened, soon proved this no
lie,
Was brought to the shambles, and then had
to die.
When, seeing the carcass hung up, then the
dog
Did never more envy the luck of a hog.

REDEEMED.

ARABIAN TALE.

A YOUTH there lived whom Fortune, oft
    called blind,
Gave all her precious gifts of form and mind,
With such a noble heart as only can
Make Heaven's fair image of a mortal man.
And everybody eagerly pretends
To love him—all profess to be his friends.
Alas! this changed. Into temptation's power
He fell, and sinned in an unguarded hour.
If keenest agony atones, then sure
Heaven hath received his contrite heart as
    pure.
But then our hypocritic, callous world
Its verdict, "Guilty," quick upon him hurled.
Each finger points at the condemned; all eyes
Frown on him, humiliating, worldly wise.
For consolation to his mates he flees;
They knew him only in his luck and glees.
One recognized him—ah! with such a face
As showed the great and condescending grace;

O'erwhelms him—fie upon it!—with the price
Of'shamming friendship, so-called good advice.
Next his affianced love bade him to go,
Inflicting on his heart most crushing blow.
Faint, writhing and convulsed, damned and
    decried,
To his parental roof he homeward hied.
Report, the ever-busy, meddling dame,
Who circulates and magnifies our shame—
She went before him. On the threshold
    stands
His agèd father, stern, with trembling hands;
He bids him, " Hence ! I've lost my son," be
    told:
" As his did mourn the Patriarch of old,
As Jacob wailed his lovèd Joseph's doom,
Uncomforted I'll go into my tomb."
The youth drops staggering; but in fond
    embrace
Is caught, and kisses deck his death-pale
    face.
With tears they're mingled, and the cry sobbed
    wild:
" Oh ! can a mother e'er forsake her child?"
Both kneel. The father, too, no longer stands
Unmoved ; he lifts and wide extends his hands,

And blesses them in pious, good old ways.
" My lost is found again !" he mildly says.
Thus was one, else from sin to crime depraved
A suicide, or worse, redeemed and saved
By that great power, equalled but Above—
A mother's tender and undying love. .

AQUA VITÆ ;

OR, THE FIRST DELIRIUM TREMENS.

KNOW ye the antique record how erst
into this world
The direst of all curses, King Alcohol, was
hurled?
And how the Fates avenged it in body, heart,
and soul
On him who first concocted th' intoxicating
bowl?

The night was dark and chilly, the storm made
heaven weep,
While all but crime and suffering were wrapt
in dreamful sleep ;

6

Then in his laboratory—yon subterranean
    space—
An Alchemist wrought misery e'er since upon
    our race.

Around, rich candelabra pale rays, blue tinted,
    shed ;
The hoary, pensive student has leaned his
    withered head
Against a solid column of cross-bones, skulls,
    and books,
While on a burnished hour-glass he has bent
    his anxious looks.

All treasures life doth offer he sacrificed as
    naught ;
His golden locks untimely are bleached by
    ceaseless thought.
For day and night he's prying into forbidden
    lore ;
He fain would solve the mystery, that death
    should be no more.

And hark ! the dome serenely aloud proclaims
    the time.
Twelve peals the echo vibrates like some
    weird, ghostly chime ;

With its last sound the student is hastening
    to and fro,
A beverage to distil and boil above the em-
    bers' glow.

'Tis the decisive moment—the midnight hour.
    On high
He lifts a brimful goblet, and spills some drops
    thereby ;
The flames are whirling, whizzing, while caba-
    listic words
He mutters, and strange signs describes, and
    hell and heaven girds.

The fire transforms its colors, a halo of sweet
    light
In which are bands of angels enveloped fair
    and bright ;
And strains of solemn music, breathed like
    Æolian strings.
A monitor of good, these words the choir
    sublimely sings :

"Touch not, lift not the poisonous cup !
    Taste not, drink not a single drop !
    Man's life is dark,
    Yet breaks a spark

Into his future, decked by night;
Faith with strong wing,
And Hope the eternal beacon-light,
From death its sting, from death its sting
Long since did sever!
This is true blessing; oh, beware!
Whoever durst
Attempt to 'scape his mortal share,
He shall be cursed! forever cursed!"

Then dies away the music and pales again
    the fire,
But in his breast burns fiercer the student's
    wild desire:
He fills anew the goblet with bold, defying mien,
The flames stirred up take human form, dark
    as the night has been.

Satire and wile and cunning are twinkling in
    his eyes;
Thus must have looked the tempter when in
    the snake's disguise.
The student even trembles and utters loud a
    shriek,
But "Silence!" bids the spirit; he thus is
    heard to speak:

" Man ! know thy father's name is lust,
    Thy mother's baptized weakness ;
They glare to Heaven, but the dust
    They'll share in perfect meekness ;
And their begotten offspring's fear,
    On Hope's sweet bosom nourished,
Led to Religion's taming bier,
    A germ dead ere it flourished.
'Tis thee ! 'tis thee ! like them thou diest,
If thou not, brave and bold, defiest
Those hands which chain thee to death's brink,
Then drink ! drink deep ! drink ever ! drink ! "

And with satanic laughter the phantom dis-
    appears.
The Alchemist is startled ; his blood and brains
    and tears
Seem melted as by fire ; he loud and wildly
    laughed,
The goblet then defiantly he emptied in one
    draught.

Without, the storm is raging ; each angry
    thunderbolt
Hurls flash on flash of lightning—a nocturnal
    black revolt ;

Then sad through night and weather sound
    like a dying moan
These words into the student's ear again, in
    plaintive tone:

  " Whoever durst
    Attempt to 'scape his mortal share,
    He shall be cursed! forever cursed!"

The draught thus won at midnight, consumed,
    its power reveals,
And, like a newly-born one, revived the old
    man feels;
At last, then, his ambition, the ideal of his
    strife,
He gloriously now has attained—th' Elixir of
    human life!

Thenceforth he has continued to mix, boil,
    and produce
The Alcohol; to his pupils he taught its make
    and use;
And with the new discovery all o'er our globe
    they went—
To castles, churches, down into the hungry
    beggar's tent.

So time passed on. Yet never from the de-
    cree of fate
Can one escape; for certain it cometh soon
    or late;
And thus, too, found the student his final,
    dreadful goal.
'Tis midnight. Hark! what screams and yells
    through storm and thunder roll!

It wakes from sleep the people, it rouses old
    and young;
Unto the laboratory bewildered masses
    throng.
And they behold with terror what man ne'er
    saw before—
The first "Delirium Tremens" there, on its
    most hideous score.

The ground, a raging maniac, his limbs in
    terror smite:
Lo! from his lips and nostrils break flames
    of purple light:
He 'gainst the block of granite his skull con-
    vulsive throws,
Until his blood, from gashing wounds, with
    brains mixed, fatal flows.

Thus died he, and was buried—none knows
    his grave or name,
But still the curse eternal has been his awful
    fame.
Where'er his poisonous beverage, the Alco-
    hol, was sent,
It sounds, from church and castle down to
    the hungry beggar's tent.

Widows, orphans, nations—all curse the hid-
    eous deed,
As mothers do and fathers whose hearts were
    made to bleed;
And children will, while hungry, and crying
    loud for bread;
The noble, good, and pure—all curse the
    memory of the dead.

Well known is yet, however, the laboratory,
    where
The dram was first discovered; 'tis still sold
    freely there.
The subterranean workshop has now been
    modernized—
Yon bar-room 'tis, across the street, so much
    by drunkards prized.

They are the student's pupils, who nightly
    congregate,
That they in drunken revels his doom per-
    petuate :
For when they stagger homeward, *sans* sense,
    and none be near,
Then it is said the maniac's ghost doth nightly
    there appear.

Through all the evolutions of the delirium
    he
Must pass, a horrid spectre, till daylight sets
    him free ;
And God in Heaven only will pardon his
    offence
When the last inebriate takes the vow of·to-
    tal abstinence.

This is the antique record, how first into the
    world
The direst of all curses, King Alcohol, was
    hurled :
And thus the Fates avenged it in body, heart,
    and soul
On him who first concocted th' intoxicating
    bowl.

7

TORTURE.

MONOLOGUE FROM DRAMA " GENIUS."

THE Buddha tells a tale which runs this
    wise :
Cruel demons will mischievously at times
Select a human being for their pranks.
They grant him all the gifts of which are.
    woven
The precious jewel, mortal happiness:
They grant him cruelly all but one ; that one
Which forms the culmination-point and centre
Of every other—the power to secure.
His prize flits by him, never near enough,
In spite of all his efforts, to be grasped.
They starve the hungry victim 'midst of plenty ;
They parch the thirsty lips in sight of foun-
    tains ;
They freeze the heart in midst of vernal sun-
    shine ;
They scorch the fevered brains in iciest winter,
Until the gods in mercy interpose

And grant him the possession of the price
Of all his direful, undeservèd suff'ring,
Or move him from such power to higher
   spheres.

THE ACCEPTED PLEDGE.

THE B'douin's keen-edged cimeter is
   As cruel as lion and tiger are.
He'll slay the men, enslave the women,
  But never has in peace or war
    His blade defiled
    By blood of child,
For surely cursed were he and his,
  Dared he to brave the mythic lore
Which every Arab knows and fears
  When Allah he heeds and dreads no more.

Thus runs pathetical the story:
  When his ancestral kindred saw
Themselves released from Egypt's bondage,
  Came unto Sinai for the law;
    'Heard was a cry
    Of voice on High:

" What hostage will these people give
  My revelation and commands
That they will cherish and obey, ,
  If I shall place them in their hands?"

Then in the council of the nation,
  The prophet great, the elders wise,
They offered memories hallowed,
  Progenitors in Paradise.
      Historic claims,
      The sainted names
Of Abram, Isaac, Israel ;
  But not sufficient were these deemed.
Birthright does not avail in Heaven :
  Each one must be himself redeemed.

In second council of the people
  They all unanimous agree
To turn bond one unto another,
  Themselves be their own guarantee.
      This sacrifice
      Would not suffice.
For they were told in language plain,
  " You are unworthy and untried—
Men who proved stiff-necked and uncouth,
  Already have the laws defied."

A third time then they met together,
" What can we offer loved and dear
Which unreserved will be accepted
　Without a doubt, without a fear?
　　What is the best,
　　All pure and blest,
Such as we cherish more than life,
　By which our hearts and souls are swept?
Our children let us offer; sure
　These Justice certain will accept."

And so it proved! The bond thus given
　Abundant was, as well it might.
The young and future generations,
　On Sinai pledged for law and right,
　　In every clime,
　　Unchanged by time,
Were sacred held by friend and foe.
　None with impunity may wrong
The children; by this solemn act,
　Unto High Heaven they all belong.

WINE.

A TALMUDICAL PARABLE.

WHEN God the grape created, every
    vine
He with a triple tincture fructified—
With blood of lion, ape, and that of swine,
  Which in the ripened juice three proper-
    ties supplied:

Drink once of wine, and you'll feel strong
    and bold,
  Combative, brave, without discrimination;
You fancy strength increased a thousand-fold,
  A sovereign king of all the animal creation.

Now drink again, and you are jolly, glad;
  You sing—it sounds like braying of a
    donkey.
You jump and laugh and caper; maudlin gad,
  Behaving like unto a veritable monkey.

Now drink once more—you'll lose all self-
    control.
  You can no longer rant, but mumble, mutter.
Unable on your feet to keep, you roll
  And wallow like a hog, low grunting in
    the gutter.

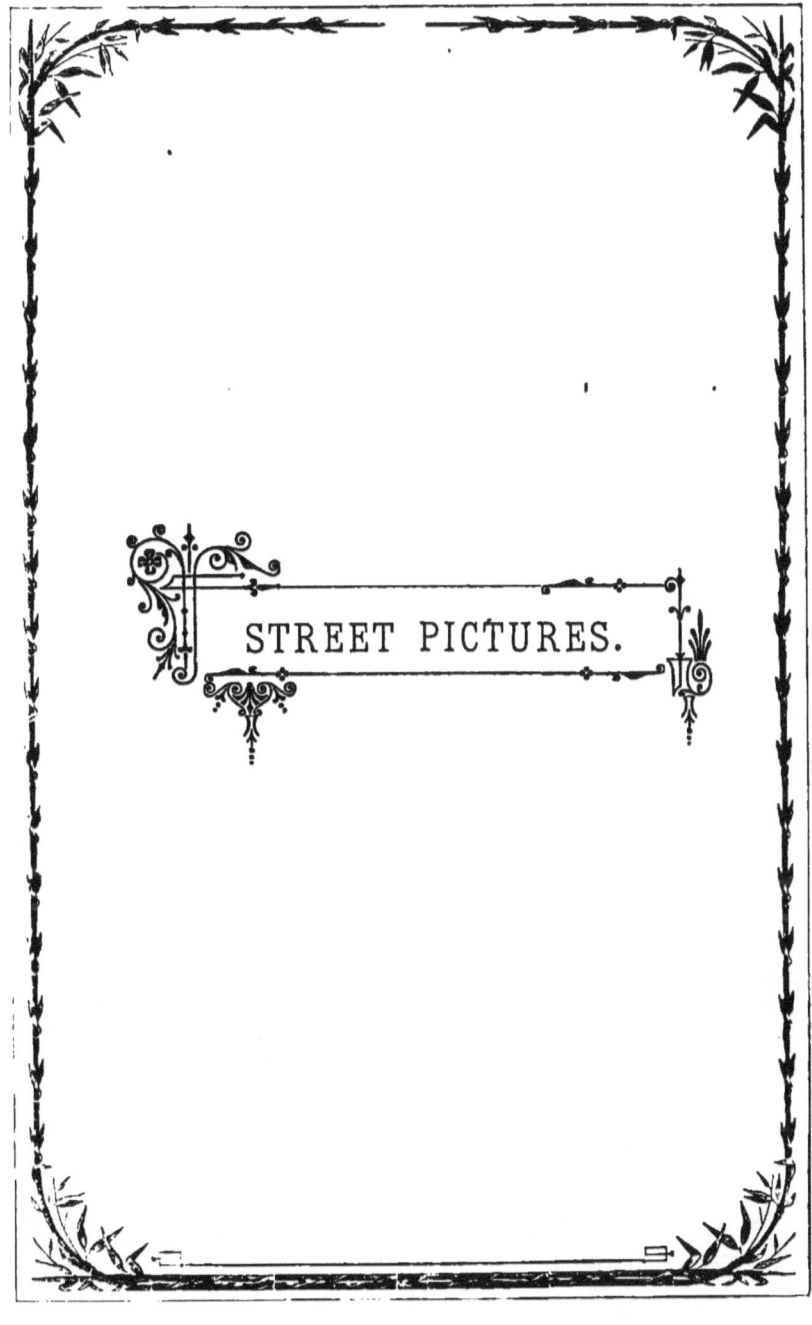

STREET PICTURES.

Street Pictures.

I.

BEHOLD! there staggers through the
busy streets
    A drunken, low, degraded one,
And every truant urchin whom he meets,
In childish sport to be molested by,
        Seems sent to cry:
        Accursed of God, reel on!

This wretch who now is trundling to his
    home,
    Alas! has lovely wife and child.
The woman, anxious, waits for him to come.
Though he maltreats, disgraces her, she yet,
        With face still wet,
        Waits for this man defiled!

8

Who is this drunkard? Of the many, one,
    With choicest gift upon his brow—
Youth, health, and mind; and these by drink
    undone.
A stain and shame to high respected ties,
    The sot thus lies
    Low in the gutter now.

There, look at him! If struck by foul disease,
    Ay, even the dread pestilence,
It could not have destroyed him with more
    ease
Than does the damnèd poison in his veins,
    Which steals his brains—
    The dram's dire consequence.

He loved her once—the woman now his wife.
    Had any other man dared make
A ruffling shadow pass upon her life,
How he would wild with indignation start!
    And now her heart
    Too true, himself does break.

He loved that babe! When born to him, at first
    With pleasure wild he wept and smiled;
Then took the boy into his arms and burst

Into a passionate, heaven-invoking prayer;
    And now his heir
He brands "the drunkard's child!"

Once his ambition soared for highest fame,
    The pride of all his friends awhile;
He long ago in rum drowned hope and name.
Delirious most, of reason near bereft,
    All for him left
Is but a lunatic's exile.

How came this doom to pass? take heed;
    come, come,
    Young friends, be warned, imbibing host!
In an unguarded moment he met some
Hilarious company—drank once—he fell
    And, clutched by hell,
Forever he was lost.

Hence, hence! I'll lead him home! Our pic-
    ture will
    O'er all the world encountered be;
Till church and school unite 'gainst bar and still.
True civilization trembles all afear,
    And drops a tear
On man's depravity!

II.

Right through the middle of the street,
In rain or sunshine, storm or sleet—
Most with bundles, with coffers some—
That's the way our "greenhorns" come.

The women are buxom, and strong the men—
German or Irish, no matter; when
They touch the ground of this free land,
Re-born are all in heart and hand.

Settling soon 'midst friends near and dear—
There are no strangers among us here.
Though some become servants and "help"
    for a time,
None are made slaves but committers of crime.

Open to all is the area of wealth—
Open to all the sources of health.
Thus many a poor one few years ago came,
Who now has attained high position and fame.

'Tis so with the emigrant women of now;
"Lis'le" becomes a fat Dutchman's frau;
Biddy is married unto her old beau—
And that is the way our "greenhorns" go!

III.

Please give me a penny! I'm hungry and
  cold!
My mother at home is sick and old.
Please give me a penny! My father has
Been in prison for weeks, alas!

He had no work, and we had no bread;
And he wished himself and all of us dead.
And then he drank liquor—it set him
  wild;
And he struck poor mother and me, his child.

When first I visited him in the cell
He hugged me so close and with such a
  yell!
And he cried and sobbed, and sobbed and
  cried,
'Midst kiss and caresses I had to chide.

So give me a penny, if you think meet,
Wherewith to buy bread for mother to eat.
Say you, sir, all this money is mine?
Thank God and bless you!—it pays father's
  fine.

I need not beg to-night any more!
We shall be happy as we were before.
And all in return I can offer to give,
You I'll remember as long as I live.

IV.

Through all the town, 'midst clatter and din,
Cries loud a voice: "Ho! who will buy sin?"

Buy sin in most hideous, repulsive guile—
Woman abandoned, degraded, and vile;

And, as she wanders to and fro,
Proclaiming: "Society made me so!"

Society, boasting of virtue sublime,
Yet pressing us creatures into crime;

Building churches, all velvet-pewed,
Yet making her daughters debased and
    lewd;

Sending the children to Sunday-school,
Then throws them into a fiery pool;

Society-dancing for charity's sake,
While lives are perishing, souls are at stake;

Robbing the masses wholesale, and then
Gives them a penny to starve in a den;

Boasting enlightenment, science, and art,
While hunger and ignorance never depart;

With all the progress but for the rich;
For the rest aye misery, prison, and ditch;

Society, meaning the moneyed folks,
While secret she fun at poverty pokes;

Marshaling 'gainst virtue the glitter of
    wealth;
Cursing the wanton she maketh by stealth.

Will ye who are guiltless now cast the first
    stone
On outcasts, who, Heaven grant, may yet
    atone?

While all through the town, 'midst clatter
    and din,
Cries loud a voice: "Ho! who will .buy
    sin?"

Buy sin in most hideous, repulsive guile—
Woman abandoned, degraded, and vile;

And, as she wanders to and fro,
Proclaiming: "Society made me so!"

V.

On the first floor in the parlor
    A lass, all youth and glee,
Sits, by her beaux surrounded—
    Young Southern chivalry.

Under her window the organ
    A one-armed soldier grinds;
The scar across his forehead
    Of battle hot, reminds.

Those up in the parlor are laughing;
  They bask in comfort and ease,
While, shivering, the invalid freezes—
  A Union-defender in peace.

The girl leans out of the window
  And throws him a coin from her hand:
"Take this; and now, old beggar,
  Come play us 'Dixie Land!'"

But through the open window
  He hurls the money back;
Then tighter the crank he clutches,
  While slowly making track.

And fast and fierce he's grinding
  The tunes of the boys in blue—
All-conquering "Yankee Doodle,"
  And "Hail Columbia" too!

A man across the corner
  Has watched the curious scene;
He knew the maimed, brave fellow—
  Had his commander been.

9

" Well done, my noble comrade!"
  And brightly shone his eyes;
" Thou shalt find home and comfort!"
  He with emotion cries.

" Here, take my hand as token:
  Long may the Union wave!"
His word has broken never—
  His general true and brave!

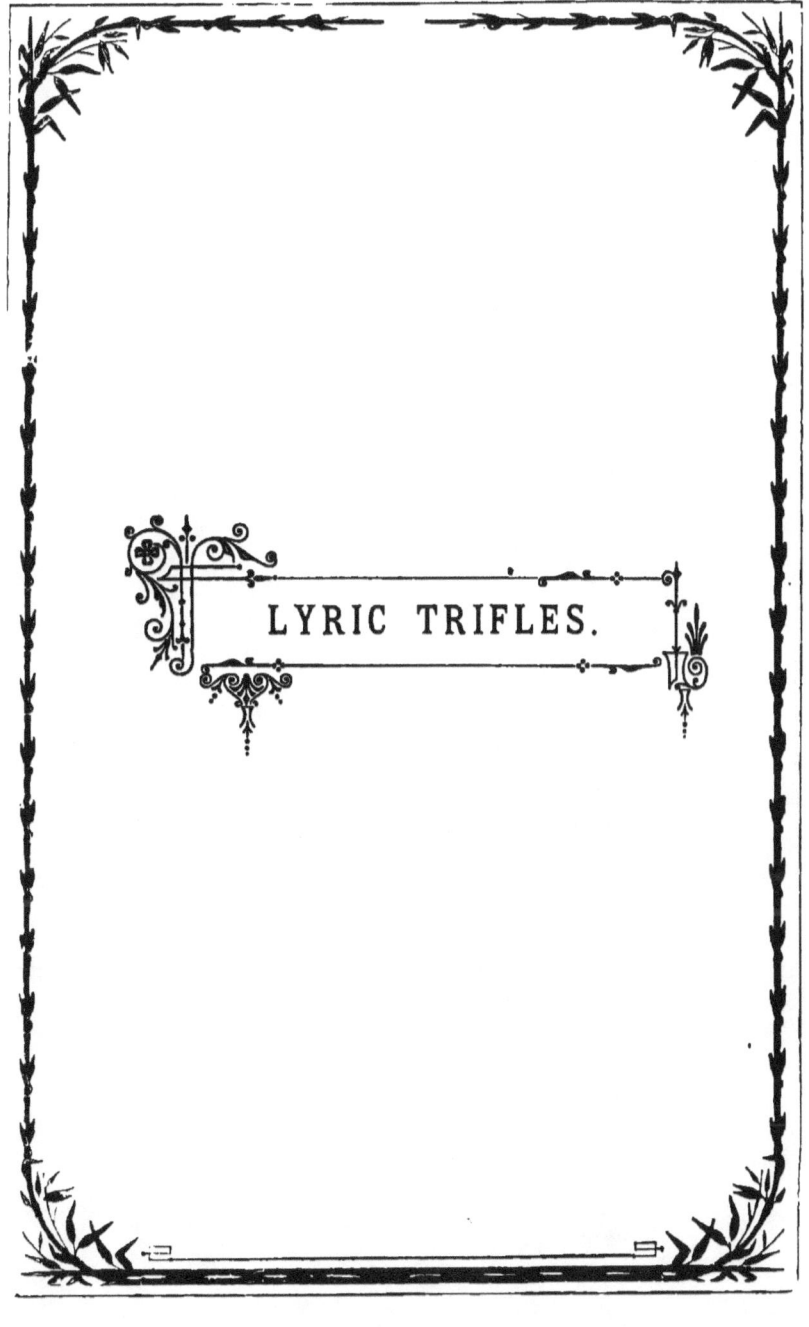

LYRIC TRIFLES.

Lyric Trifles.

SONNET.

DISSONANCE and Harmony combined
Form that sweet music which unlocks
   our soul
And makes the ear feast under its control.
Thus is the heart, too, touched, if we can find
The poet's song, conveying to our mind
Word music. Alternately should roll
The tears of woe and anguish copious flow-
   ing,
Dissolved by sparkling wit and joy all glow-
   ing.

My songs were culled in such varieties
Of wine and love, intrigue and merry glees.
Alas! I hear the living and the dying
Cry loud for help and see all the degrees
Of misery in all its stages. Denying
Me all—but dissonance and grating melodies.

IN MEMORIAM.

ADOLPH CRÉMIEUX, LIFE SENATOR OF FRANCE.

Y ISGADAL w'yiskadash!*
    The Hebrew's mourning prayer—
Resounds in temple and synagogue;
For Time, the cruel slayer,
Laid fatal hand upon a chief.
All Isr'el is in tears and grief.
As Rachel mourns her lost—a mother—
We Crémieux mourn—our brother.

Yisgadal w'yiskadash!
Religion feels extending,
Wherever people worship God,
The woful loss, heartrending.
Alike for Gentile and for Jew
A great man left us—good and true.
Religion, like bereft a mother,
She Crémieux mourns—our brother.

Yisgadal w'yiskadash!
Law, Justice loud are wailing.
Oppressed of every land and clime
May well feel faint and failing.

* "Be exalted and sanctified." The beginning words of the Hebrew
prayer for the dead, called "Kadish."

For Freedom lost one of her stays
When death cut short his mortal days.
Truth sorrows like a stricken mother
Crémieux is dead—our brother.

Yisgadal w'yiskadash!
Humanity in anguish
"Reste in pace!" trembling weeps,
Nor soon her woe will languish.
For God hath stilled a human heart
In which the whole world had a part.
Humanity, our common mother,
Weeps Crémieux!—weeps our brother!

JUDGE NOT, CONDEMN NOT.

JUDGE not, condemn not! Men who
are accused   .
Often are guiltless and cruelly abused.
Error is quick, restitution comes slow;
Be not foremost the first stone to throw.
Time enough, time enough guilt to de-
plore!
Judge not—wait till the trial is o'er!

Often appearances tend to betray,
Often passions our judgment sway,
Often is innocence foully assailed—
Truth is naked, while falsehood is mailed;
Honor once taken you cannot restore.
Judge not—wait till the trial is o'er!

Ere the fair fame of a brother you doom,
Ponder as if you stood over his tomb;
Dip it in kindness, steep it in love;
Handle it tenderly—think of Above!
Judge not, condemn not! 'twas bidden of
       yore.
Judge not—wait till the trial is o'er.

THINK OF IT.

THINK of it! our joy and sorrow
     Of the present, of the morrow,
Love and hate, and hope and fear,
Friends afar or e'er so near,
All must die to live!—'tis writ.
Think of it, Oh! think of it.

Think of it! then let no trouble
E'er attempt its share to double.
Think of it, and let no joy
Time of more importance cloy.
All must die to live!—'tis writ.
Think of it, Oh! think of it.

Think of it! for all affection
Cannot stay its deep deflection;
Nor may hatred at the best
Time in his due course arrest.
All must die to live!—'tis writ.
Think of it, Oh! think of it.

Think of it! when fearing, hoping—
We're not e'er in darkness groping.
Those afar or e'er so near—
Think of it and never fear:
All must die to live!—'tis writ.
Think of it, Oh! think of it.

IN MEMORIAM.

WILLIAM CULLEN BRYANT.

WEEP, nation of America—mourn, all
the world!
A man whose fame around humanity is furled,
A great, good man, is dead! His life had
been anointed,
A bard and seer, by the hand of God appointed;

His words and thoughts and deeds harmonious pearled
As one great poem, most sublimely wrought
and jointed,
A never-dying song contained in this syn-
opsis—
The ever-living, the immortal "Thanatopsis!"

Thy native country, thy beloved fatherland,
For one like unto thee who all revered, departs,
Has but one Pantheon! It must be beauti-
fully grand
To be enshrined forever in loving, human
hearts.

Among the best and noblest thou hast been
  a giant!
" Requiescat in pace!" This tear for
  WILLIAM CULLEN BRYANT.

NECRODULIE.

AN ACROSTIC.

HENRY WADSWORTH LONGFELLOW.

H ÚSH! the heart is stilled that rang
    E ver warm for truth and right;
N ow the voice is dead that sang
R oyally for life and light—
Y ea, for all that's grand and bright!

W eep! our foremost bard is gone!
A ll reluctantly and prone
D ead to realize him ever;
S ong and light and truth; who never
W ove but what was most sublime.
O de of grief! a mournful chime,
R inging o'er the country, tolling;
T ear-inviting, unconsoling—
H iawatha's author gone!

Lo! from out his pall and tomb—
Oh! these very words are gloom—
Ne'ertheless breaks forth a vision,
Glorious true, a poet's mission.
For all ages, ever vernal,
Ever youthful and in bloom;
Life's memorial, God's commission:
Light and Truth and Song eternal
Orb and crown his life and name
With immortal, God-like fame!

THE DEAD RABBI.

*IN MEMORY OF THE LATE LAMENTED REV. DR. MAX
LILIENTHAL, OF CINCINNATI.*

THE grave is filled and the crowds are
    gone;
The solemn obsequies are past.
The Rabbi is dead, and buried, and sleeps,
    Reposing forever and aye at last.
From early youth till his green old age
    He cared not for quiet, he sought not for
      rest.

His was the battle for knowledge and truth;
A man of the sturdiest, grandest, and
best—
A laborer and sage
In our time and age.
His was the struggle for right and light,
To set the oppresséd and bonded free;
To teach to his people, advancing the world:
"Nearer, my God, to Thee, nearer to
Thee."

As time shall roll on they'll erect him a shaft
Of bronze or Carrarian marble white.
With golden letters it will hold inscribed
His life and death so pure and bright.
But needed are scarcely the metal or stone—
The task he achieved shall time defy;
For thought is immortal and mind has no end,
And Love, Hope, and Charity never will die.
Invisibly kept,
Are tears sadly wept;
The ache of the heart and the anguish of souls
Exist for eternity, floating on,
Until humanity's mission is reached
And earth and time their work have done.

A life thus completed, a labor thus wrought,
    A goal thus achieved which divinely was
      born,
A day thus closed and an eve thus begun,
    Must have after nightfall again a morn.
There must be a waking from such a dream;
    There will be a rising after such sleep.
Nothing in nature does really die:
    The world shall not mourn forever and
      weep.

      Ah, sorrow no more!
      It was written of yore:
" The dust shall return·unto mother earth,
    But home the Lord our souls will call."
The name of the righteous shall ever be
    blessed—
    Then rest in peace, RABBI LILIENTHAL.

THE SONG OF THE JEWELER.

A BALLAD.

I'VE been commissioned to make this
thing—
A wedding-ring, a wedding-ring;
And while I melt and mould this gold
My lay is short and quickly told.

The maid to wear this band so fine—
She loved me, promised to be mine.
It is the story old as time,
Rehearsed in prose and sung in rhyme:

Since he is rich and I am poor,
She now forsakes me, perjured sure.
Into this crucible I'd melt
The pangs I feel, the pangs I felt.

It is the hardest work, I con,
I'll ever do, I've ever done;
The sadder all, that with this ring
I'd pray, that happiness it bring.

No matter, though, how hard my fate,
All scorn and hate, all scorn and hate,
Within my heart they take their flight
If she'll this circlet cherish right.

God bless the ring, the sign sublime!
My hammer and my anvil chime!
And " Amen " shall my true love say
To-morrow on her wedding-day.

ADIEU, ADIEU! I GAVE THEE UP.

A DIEU, adieu! I gave thee up
     With bleeding heart and quiver-
        ing soul,
And from a blasted hope this drop—
A tear, I'm not ashamed of—roll.
Yes! thou wast very dear to me ;
I happy dreamed to be with thee.
Thy and my fate I but bewail
That thou should be so fair and frail,
And that I loved, one more loved never,
And now must give thee up forever.

TO THE MEMORY OF A DEPARTED
FRIEND.

WHOEVER was able unraveling life,
　　With all its great joy and great
　　sorrow,
With all its ambition, loves, hopes, and strife
　　And the cares we borrow?
When barely begun we end our career
To leave love, hope, and ambition here.

Whoever was able unfathoming death,
　　Who comes 'midst tears and heart-aching;
Closing dear eyes and quenching loved breath,
　　No station forsaking?
The rich and the poor, the lowly, the great,
Are equally meeting the certain fate.

'Tis all a blank mystery, all wrapt in night!
　　With only this high consolation:
Humanity, goodness, love, honor, and right,
　　Our immortal creation,
Like Heaven eternal, like God, know no end!
Requiescat in pace! my noble, good friend.

II

NIL DESPERANDUM.

I.

THE poorest thing on earth to life doth
      cling;
  .And I—must I despair?
My heart is quivering, feverish, in each string
    'Tis sore with grief and care.
    To Heaven I stare,
Praying *sans* hope; the eye filled with a tear—
Within the breast a sting—the soul all fear.

II.

When I was yet a child,
    Roaming and wild,
I often dreamt many a dream so bright,
    By day and night.
But youth has vanished, all dreams are gone,
Like bubbles that into thin air are blown.

All that life hath brought
    To manhood wrought
Is but ceaseless, fruitless toil
    And wild turmoil.
And this for enough of bread but to reap,
To feel the hunger that banishes sleep.

Would I were yet a child,
  Roaming wild,
And dreaming that beautiful vision once more
  That upward bore
The innocent boy to the spheres of light,
Never again to wake from that night!

III.

And still, the poorest thing to life doth cling;
  Nor will I yet despair.
The heart may quiver, feverish, in each string,
  Sore with grief and care.
  To Heaven I stare!
And, praying, hope returns; it dries the tear;
The sting has lost its pangs, the soul all fear.

I THINK OF THEE, I THINK OF THEE.

MIDNIGHT THOUGHTS.

I THINK of Thee, I think of Thee!
    While shivering midnight decks the
    world.
I think of Thee, I think of Thee,
    Though in sleep's cloak the earth is furled.
Oh! slumber Thou, sweet dreams be thine,
While sad, alone, and 'wake I pine.

I think of Thee, I think of Thee!
    Through storm and rain yon blinks one
    star.
I think of Thee, I think of Thee:
    Like midnight thus my feelings are.
I think of thee: Thou like that spark
Shed'st light into my bosom dark.

I think of Thee, I think of Thee,
    He who made darkness, storm, and rain.
I think of Thee, I think of Thee—
    Brings morning, too, to soothe our pain.
May He protect us in His might!
I think of Thee. Good-night—good-night.

TO LOVE AND BE LOVED IN RETURN.

TO love and be loved in return!
O Heaven! what rapture is con-
tained
In this one sentiment—the bourne
Of bliss and blessing. Unrestrained
By all that is of mortal birth,
It makes a paradise of earth.

To love and be loved! It implies
Intensest passion, pure and kind;
One that ennobles, sanctifies
The human heart and soul and mind.
Whom is assigned such destiny,
Though poor, is rich; though low, stands
high.

To love and be loved! To your heart
Hold pressed the precious gift, and then
May fortune smile, or vile depart.
Above this all stand loving men.
Their faith and hope here and Above
It is to be loved and to love.

TO LOVE IN VAIN—WHAT AGONY!

WHAT agony—to love in vain!—
    Is not implied by these few words,
When yearning woe will not restrain
    The harrowed breast in all its cords?
The feverish blood leaps through the veins,
As if to madden soul and brains.

True! we feel sad to part with friends,
    Yet may we hope to meet again.
But no such consolation sends
    Love unreturned—a love in vain.
It does imply the saddest doom,
A checkered life, an early tomb.

True, true! we mourn when, severed by
        death,
    Goes home one who to us is dear;
But we believe with our last breath
    Of an hereafter's higher sphere.
The heart, alas! here and Above
Despairs of when 'tis broke by love.

SONG.

FROM THE DRAMA "GENIUS."

'NEATH coral, shell, and weed the
    ocean
One priceless pearl conceals:
Thus hides my heart a deep emotion,
    The fervent love it feels.

On Heaven's vaulted blue, unmeasured,
    One sun holds high control:
Thus is thine radiant picture treasured
    Supremely in my soul.

'Tis said, of solar light depriven,
    The gem would surely die:
So must my love and life be riven
    Were closed to me thine eye.

Then as the sun, whenever shining,
    Reflects him in the sea,
Deign thou unto my soul repining
    One look of sympathy.

SONG.

FROM THE DRAMA " SAMSON."

AND must I then not love thee?
　Thou art not of my creed!
So help the Lord above me,
　I can and will not heed!
'Tis vain indeed forever
　Affection pure to part;
For naught true love can sever
　From a beloved heart.

I climbed the mountain lonely;
　The solitude above
With silent tongue asked only:
　"What creed forbids to love?"
I walked the sea-shore, musing;
　The surf beneath, indeed,
Sang evermore, accusing:
　"Love cares not for a creed."

Where'er I roamed I met thee;
　'Tis vain—I'll not forsake.
For ere I could forget thee
　My heart must surely break.

'Tis vain indeed forever
   Affection pure to part;
For naught true love can sever
   From a beloved heart.

FOURTH OF JULY, 1861.

THIS is a day which the Lord has ap-
    pointed.
  Open the chapels, and, kneeling devout,
Glory to Him who our heroes anointed,
  Strengthening their hearts, brave, noble,
    and stout,
To rescue the Nation from tyranny
On Liberty's birthday, the Fourth of July.

God of our fathers! Who ever hast guarded,
  In battle and council, America's fate,
Hear, we invoke Thee! restore the departed
  Peace, love, and freedom to every State.
May proudly the eagle soar high to the sky
On Liberty's birthday, each Fourth of July.

12

OTHER POEMS.

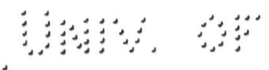
Other Poems.

YAH, YAH!*

A TEUTONIC SKETCH.

I.

A PICTURESQUE village on the banks of
the Rhine,
With crimson-hued oak and the well-loaded
vine;
A cottage all decked in moss, ivy, and green,
Though crumbling, yet cheerful and cozy
and clean,
Is the home of a silver-haired widow—" Yah,
yah,"
But her only son's in America!

* *Yah, yah !*—Yes, yes !

In a snowy-white cap and an old-fashioned
    gown
  She sits in the huge old family chair;
Her face it is wrinkled, her form is bent down,
    And her fine Roman nose holds a spec-
      tacle pair.
'Tis twilight; she's knitting, and oft sighs,
    "Yah, yah,
How my heart yearns for him in America!

"He writes of that fair and beautiful land,
And of things we old folks can't understand.
That all there are equal, and all there are
    free,
And labor is honored in the land o'er the
    sea."
With cracked and with tremulous voice she
    adds, " Yah,
God prosper and bless America!"

As mesh upon mesh her worsted-work grows
  The embers die out in the quaint rustic
    grate;
She drowsily nods and sinks in repose,
  But sudden is roused by the creaky-
    hinged gate.

Knocks the postman. A letter! She cries
    out: " Yah,
It comes from my boy in America!"

She would not exchange it for jewel or
    charm.
With fumbling finger and trembling arm,
And while with emotion beats quicker her
    heart,
She opens the missive, and reads, with a start,
And a tear, and a smile, loud rejoicing—
    " Yah, yah,
He's well, he's well in America!"

"He's coming!" "I'm here!" cries a voice.
    By the sound
  She knows him—she knows him—and,
    speechless with joy,
Her arms his weather-bronzed neck clasp
    around,
  And her head drops reclining on the breast
    of her boy.
But then she recovers, and sobs out, " Yah,
    yah,
My child, oh! my son from America!"

II.

"And do you know my Fritz has come—
Gretchen, his sweetheart,. to take to his
    home?
Valley and mountain, ocean and State,
Never true loving hearts separate!
And when his young 'Frau'* he takes over
    the sea,
Their wrinkled old mother—they'll never
    leave me;
They beg and entreat incessant: 'Yah, yah,'
I must with them go to America.

"Seventy years—aye, seventy years—
With tears and with smiles, with hopes and
    with fears,
With joys and with sorrows, have come and
    have gone:
Happily married, left widowed alone;
Yon in God's-acre sleep husband and child,
Father and mother! It makes me quite wild
To place the ocean between us—'Yah, yah,'
And die and be buried in America.

* *Frau*—Wife.

"To leave my cottage, my flowers and vines,
And every dear object my bosom enshrines;
Old neighbors and friends, with daughters
       and sons—
'Grossmutter'* all call me the little ones;
My birds and my chickens, and Tabby, the
       cat—
Farewell to say now to this and to that.
Oh! how my poor heart will ache, 'Yah,
       yah,'
To part with them now for America!

"But there will be all the loved ones of mine,
And there the sun as here will shine;
And something better there, too, will be:
A blessed country where all are free!
Nor do I doubt, nor do I fear,
That over the ocean, God, too, is near.
All days of my life I trusted Him. 'Yah,
He'll never forsake me in America!

"So gladly I say, then, His will be done!
'Yah,' I will go with you, my daughter and
       son.

* *Grossmutter*—Grandmother.

13

Get ready, get married; be blessed! And
    you know
We'll be there the sooner, the sooner we
    go.
I fancy already—I talk like the old—
Some darling wee babe, eh? on my knees I
    may hold;
Then I will be ready to die — ' Yah, yah,
    yah '—
To sleep my last sleep in America.

III.

"Five years it is since I've sailed over the
    brine,
Exchanging the Mississippi in place of the
    Rhine.
Else nothing has altered—the ivy and green
Deck cosy my cottage, as yonder has been.
With more than childlike affection and grace
Was modeled my New by my Old World
    place.
And neighbors and friends I have found—
    ' Yah, yah '—
Loving and kind, too, in America!

" Still something has changed: more weak and
    frail
My body is growing. I visibly fail
In health and strength, in speech and song:
But spite of all I feel again young,
In children's children, youth and life,
My noble son and his darling wife,
Their dark-faced boy and fair-haired girl—
    ' Yah,'
It seems like a dream in America!

" With never a sorrow, with never a care,
Most blessed of mothers—enough and to spare,
For wants and for charity yields the good farm.
All hearts here are tender — so strong every
    arm!
Dependent alone on each other for love,
And goodness and mercy on Him who's
    Above.
Around me is blooming the sunny South—
    ' Yah,'
My old age is blessed in America!

" The mocking-bird warbles so cheer'ly his
    tune;
Magnolia and roses perfume the sweet June;

Around me reigns peace serenely and mild,
While rocking to sleep the darling, dear child.
My thoughts, though, will wander, my tears
    freely flow,
As over the ocean to the Rhineland they go.
I weep for my dear ones there buried—'Yah,
    yah,'
Our dead friends abroad live in America.

"But still I am thankful that I have been
    spared
To witness such joy, and such happiness reared.
My heart is so full, I must fall on my knees:
I thank Thee, O Lord, Who my innermost
    sees,
For all Thy great mercy! Soon wilt Thou,
    I know,
Permit me to see Thee—I'm ready to go!
But with my last breath I shall breathe it:
    'Yah, yah,'
God bless thee and prosper, America!

"And when they shall lay me away in my
    grave,
Let the Father of Rivers my resting-place
    lave.

Where life was so tranquil, there cannot be
    room
For aught but for hope, love, and faith in
    the tomb.
Rose and magnolia plant over it bright;
On modest memorial this epitaph write:
, 'Here rests a true woman from Germany,
    "Yah,"
Who lived and died blessing America!'"

BANKRUPT.

A PICTURE OF THE TIMES.

OUT of the thousands but few peruse
    One petit item, scarce more than a line,
Next editorial or telegraph news;
    Typed—it is almost for reading too fine—
Making report of some business encumber'd,
Such as appear now uncounted, unnumber'd.

"Bankrupt" it heralds a mercantile firm
    Somewhere up in a country town.
Well, who does care if another must squirm?
    Old is the story of life up and down;

But while it seems, ah! one more bursted
    bubble,
Fathom who can, its heartache and trouble.

Suffering and tears of the man who has failed,
    One already advanced in years--
He who never from hardships has quailed,
    Never knew selfishness, cringing, or fears.
Weary long years he has labored and striven,
Building the fortune a moment has riven.

Highly respected and honored his fame,
    Bond made his word with all whom he
        dealt;
Unquestioned credit attached to his name;
    Wealthy and poor a friend in him felt.
Wife and children his home happy render—
Loving, beloved, kind, generous, and tender.

Bankrupt now, and helpless involved!
    Caused by the unforeseen crisis; betrayed
Sadly by those whom he trusted; resolved—
    Honestly facing his doom undismayed—
All that he owns in this world, to his lend-
        ers
Scrupulously and fully surrenders.

Bankrupt! Now do you know what it is,
   Blighting one of his sensitive sort?—
One who never knew want such as this,
   One to whom loved ones look up for support;
Penniless, houseless, friendless, despairing,
Hopelessly into the dark future staring.

Look at the contrast! Affluence and ease
   Changed into poverty, actual need—
Barely enough common wants to appease.
   Pride is alone, and that shame, indeed,
Left him, that natural shrinking feeling
Which from the world his woe is concealing.

Winter approaches, and there is no fuel;
   Hunger is gnawing, and there is no bread;
Children are naked—O God! 'tis too cruel:
   An invalid wife confined to her bed.
Hark! How he shrieks! insane! How he
   cowers!
"Spare them, O Lord! Upon me fall Thy
   powers!"

Thus is struck down the cultured, refined,
   By a commercial tidal wave.
Easy the end can be told or defined:
   Broken, a heart fills a newly-made grave.

Widow and orphans are weeping and wailing—
Father of Mercy, oh! be Thou not failing.

SUNSET ON MOUNT DAVIDSON.*

1865.

MOUNTAIN-CONE, upon thy summit,
   where the North wind icy blows,
In the dying evening twilight, dying like a
   full-blown rose,
Lingers one beholding wonders more sublime eyes never saw:
Steep the hillsides, deep the valleys—landscape
   picture without flaw.

Miles above the ocean-level, isolated from the
   world,
Sterile, only heather growing, and the sage-
   brush thickly curled—
Rarefied, the air can barely breath supply—
   still here attests
Every knoll that human labor ne'er is daunted,
   never rests.

* Virginia City and Gold Hill, Nev., lie at the foot of Mt. Davidson.

One decade ere this the Indian roamed alone
    here, digging root;
Now see palaces of granite dot the country
    black with soot;
Instead of wigwam and of camp-fire rolls the
    flame of coal and pines
From the mouth of steam-machinery through
    the densely peopled mines.

As if by a dream created, or as by some
    magic spell,
Roads and houses, hamlets, cities, gird the
    hill and grace the dell.
High up into the Sierra, who the wond'rous
    sight beholds,
Far away to Utah's desert, where the Salt-
    Lake growls and scolds:

Yes, as high as sight will carry, and as low
    as travel sound,
Pick and axe have shaft and tunnel hewn into
    the rock and ground;
For since Nature, always loving, clothed the
    surface all in dearth,
She has planted richest treasures in the
    bowels of the earth.

14

Deep below, the virgin-metal joyous weds
    with Industry—
Thus is close the far-off Northland joined to
    Civilization nigh.
People leave their homes and country, flock
    to places waste and sere—
They are coming, coming, coming, spite of
    hardship, risk, and fear ;

Coming like a new migration, traveling on
    the wings of steam—
A reality which shortly seemed but like a
    maniac's scheme ;
Telegraph and locomotive, electric wire and
    iron track,
Modern knights, jumped on the giant, on
    old Rocky Mountain's back.

Every day brings new processions; thus they
    pour in file by file ;
They find room, find peace and plenty, find
    a home. Perhaps you smile ;
But the watchword of the Nations, worthy
    of the present day,
Liberty's parole is: *"Ubi bene ibi patria !"* *

* Wherever I fare well, there is my home.

TICONDEROGA CENTENNIAL.

1775—*MAY* 10—1875.

THERE stands many a castle-ruin in other
far-off climes.
The traveler looks in wonder, reminded of
bygone times—
Reminded of horror and terror of bonds, and
fetters and slaves,
Of untold tyrant-oppression and despots' un-
known graves.

How different sounds the story, like song's
undying strain,
From the Ruins of Ticonderoga, on beautiful
Lake Champlain !
The very place is holy, and sanctified each
mound ;
A monument is each wall-stone, on consecrated
ground.

It speaks of a Nation rising and hewing in
twain its yoke,
Wielding a giant's weapon with death-defy-
ing stroke.

It speaks of Freedom's natal, proclaiming in
    its throe
The birth of the Republic one hundred years
    ago.

" *In the name of the* GREAT JEHOVAH ! " was
    made the stern demand,
" *And the Continental Congress !* " by Ethan
    Allen's band.
It opened to the summons, the foreigner moved
    out,
While freemen took possession with glorious
    Yankee shout.

Immortal be the story, like song's undying
    strain—
The Ruins of Ticonderoga, on beautiful Lake
    Champlain.
The place be ever holy, and sanctified each
    mound ;
A monument each wall-stone, on consecrated
    ground.

SERIOUS MISTAKE.

FOR pencil or chisel it would be a
    scene,
Could artist or sculptor but present have
    been—
A tableau that would have established their
    fame,
To paint or to model the ancient dame.

Behold her there sitting in grandfather's
    chair,
Wrinkled and withered, in silver-bleached
    hair,
The spectacles her well-pointed nose squeeze,
The family Bible lies on her knees.

And there she reads of the first man's birth,
How God creates Adam from dust of the
    earth.
But hold! here she stops; the page is all
    done :
Over she turns, but two leaves instead one.

Serene she continues, and never does mark
This turning has gone in old Noah's new
    Ark.
And thus she proceeds, with voice cracked
    and thin :
" He covered with pitch both outside and
    in ! "

Imagine who can her face, mouth, and eyes !
If lightning had struck her from Heaven's
    blue skies,
Bewildered, astonished she could not be
    more.
One jump, and erect she stands straight on
    the floor.

And then she exclaims : " I'm three-score and
    one,
But never did dream how frail we were
    done.
La, mercy ! man made out of dust of the
    ditch,
And ' kivered ' all inside and outside with
    pitch ! "

WASHINGTON'S JUDGMENT.

A VISION. [1861.]

YON, where the Potomac winds its course
round Vernon's holy height,
I've seen the spirit of Washington rise in
my dream at night;
The hero blest,
Who stood the test
Of trying time, no more can rest;
Aroused by dreadful battle-cry with which
his children rave—
The sons unworthy of their sires—it woke
him from his grave.

The Continental chief, he stands, yon on the
topmost hill;
His right hand holds the sword high raised,
the tears of sorrow fill
His eyes; thus may
He've looked that day
When foes held o'er the country sway;
When he did life and honor pledge to his
own native land,
The Father of his country, 'midst that noble,
stalwart band—

Aye, this, his own, his native land, for which
    he fought and bled,
The pride and glory of our globe e'er since
    his arm it led;
        The hallowed sod
        With brother's blood
    Is red, and into dust is trod.
That glorious banner 'neath which he, as if
    by Heaven's power,
Victoriously the Delaware ·crossed, in that
    self-same hour.

America's Constitution!—this, our modern
    Bible, torn,
This sacred patrimony decked with hatred,
    guilt, and scorn;
        The verdant tree
        Of Liberty,
    Beneath whose shadow all were free,
Leaf-stripped, and by the dreadful storm
    which from the Southward blows,
Columbia's hero no longer more finds in his
    tomb repose.

Yon, where the Potomac winds its course
    round Vernon's holy height,

I've seen the spirit of Washington rise in
    my dreams at night:
      The hero brave
      From out his grave,
    By his own sons dishonored, gave
His judgment, awful and serene, like ancient
    prophecy:
That odious, hated, and accursed all traitors
    surely be.

"Fugitives and vagabonds! like Cain's shall
    be their dooms;
Branded and marked like him, free soil
    shall ne'er contain their tombs;
      A by-word and
      Example stand
    For coming eras in every land;
Their country's woe, their children's curse,
    and their ancestors' shame,
Thus shall America's history preserve hence-
    forth their name."

Thus cried aloud George Washington. The
    morning dawned afar;
Shrill sounded fife and drum, and all the
    circumstance of war.

15

I, 'midst the roar,
Saw Heavenward soar
An eagle who a rattlesnake bore:
And then awoke; but could not help—
I thought this dream must be
A vision which rebellion judged, like an-
cient prophecy.

THE WHITEWASH-BRUSH.

THE whitewash-brush, the whitewash-
brush,
Is higher than Allah, greater than "Josh";
In letters and science, in commerce and art,
It plays its wondrous, powerful part;
Aye! all its haughty compeers are bosh
Compared to the mighty whitewash-brush.

Commanded by influence or gold,
It is the protector of young and old.
Every department of modern life
Reeking with wickedness and strife,
Society, politics, religion—hush!
They are all safe 'neath the whitewash-brush.

Scandal and gossip, the signs of our time,
Petty sin and unheard-of crime,
Judge and president, priest and flock,
May boldly at public opinion mock;
Whatever the peril, let them rush
And hide in the shade of the whitewash-
    brush.

With a few quick strokes it covers shames,
Paints all fairly the blackest of names;
Investigation it renders short
With a friendly committee's swift report;
And behold, instead of the sinner's crush,
A coat laid on by the whitewash-brush!

All other emblems, then, let us lay down—
The cross and the sword, the mitre and
    crown;
Nor learning, nor justice, nor faith should
    miss
To take for their standard a sign like this,
Without a scruple, without a blush:
The gilded sign of a whitewash-brush!

NEIR TOMID.*

*A HEBREW LEGEND FROM THE CHRONICLES OF THE
CITY OF WORMS.*

OLD Worms, the Teuton's stronghold,
    close buckled to the Rhine,
Shows yet the massive synagogue with its
    time-hallowed shrine;
There burn two lamps for ever, the chronicle
    does state—
A most mysterious legend, which they still
    perpetuate.

And thus is told the story: It chanced in
    times of yore,
When history its gloomiest fruit of blood
    and carnage bore;
The Jews were then the objects of hatred
    and disdain,
Denounced by hypocritic priests, by blinded
    people slain.

* Lamps burned constantly in memory of a beloved dead.

Fanatics, well supported with superstition's aid,
Against Worms' congregation raised a cruel,
    dangerous raid.
" The public wells are poisoned," report first
    whispers shy ;
" The public wells are poisoned ! " soon goes
    forth the dreadful cry.

" They who of old our Saviour with malice
    crucified
Now caused the pestilence by which so
    many Christians died ;
Their Rabbins have been loitering suspi-
    ciously around,
And in their cursed Ghetto are all yet well
    and sound."

The streets are filled with people e'er ready
    for a row.
" Hepp, hepp ! " * they cry ; and " Kill the
    Jews ; they are damned anyhow ! "
Into the threatened quarter the raging
    masses sped ;
The frightened outcasts quick into the syna-
    gogue they fled.

* A cry of doubtful origin, used by the mobs in Germany preceding and
during Jewish persecutions.

Upon their knees are lying men, women,
    young and old,
All weeping, wrapt into their shrouds, most
    awful to behold;
They're solemnly reciting their dismal, dying
    chants,
While for their blood the riot fierce with-
    out loud cries and pants:

" The cabalists, the criminals, we of your
    hands require,
Doomed in the holy Roman realm to death
    upon the pyre!
If you withhold our bidding, or to resist
    connive,
We'll burn forthwith the Ghetto—aye, we'll
    roast you all alive!"

The elders and the people for counsel quick
    combine,
Their hoary teachers praying on before the
    holy shrine.
Loud sounds their "Sh'ma Israel"* into
    each ear and heart;
Crowbar and axe outside attempt the door
    to break or part.

* The leading Hebrew prayer.

"These walls are strong—a fortress in this
    our time of need ;
Our wives and children we'll defend, and,
    if God hath decreed,
We'll die here with our teachers, like heroes
    and like men :
Do like the Maccabeans — arm ! arm for re-
    sistance then ! "

All rush now to the portals with death-
    defying will.
But hark ! outside the noise subsides ; it
    suddenly grows still ;
The port-bolts give, and by themselves the
    doors are open cast.
Hence flies the startled, boisterous mob ; all
    danger, sure, is past.

The vestibule is lighted, and unconsumed,
    like spells,
The faggots burn, as once the bush of which
    the Bible tells ;
And where the flames lick topmost the pyres
    in purple sheen,
Two agèd men are standing firm, by all the
    people seen.

They had come, none knew whither, and
    loudly did exclaim
Unto the furious Christians: "Stay! we are
    alone to blame!
Shed not the blood that's innocent; on us
    may fall your ire!"
Forthwith the stack is kindled; they are
    doomed unto the fire.

But lo! the flame ne'er singes upon their
    heads a hair;
Erect they stand, with upraised hands: their
    persecutors stare
In frenzied consternation unto the awful
    sight;
And terror 'smites fanatics wild, who take,
    confused, to flight.

The Israelites, too, see there the miracle
    declared
By which the hour of danger thus has
    passed and they are spared;
They still cry: "Sh'ma Israel!" Behold,
    the embers feared
Die out at once, and suddenly the two men
    disappeared.

They vanished, none knew whither; but
    from that day till now
Before the tabernacle were, as a most sa-
    cred vow,
By day and night kept burning — thus is
    each sexton bid—
Two lamps, denominated well the martyrs'
    " Neir Tomid ! "

Old Worms, the Teuton's stronghold, close
    buckled to the Rhine,
Shows yet the massive synagogue with its
    time-hallowed shrine ;
And with its two lamps burning, the chroni-
    cle does state—
This most mysterious legend, which they
    still perpetuate.

FEBRILE FRENZIES.

FANTASIA.

I.

I TOSS abed in fever craze,
   Clam perspiration decks my face;
And ugly visions rise and strain
My burning, throbbing, aching brain.

Nor sleep nor wake, as one who dies,
Wide glaring, open stand my eyes;
And soon in cataleptic throes
Methinks are fading hopes and woes.

Dim pass away my thoughts and songs,
Whate'er the heart loves, fears, and longs;
And, like a fleeting shadow stray,
Life ebbs oblivious soon away.

The people come, the people go;
Some turn me over to and fro;
My body in a coffin crowd,
Clean washed, and clothed in linen shroud.

By usage old, which yet prevails,
Six unplaned boards, box-shaped with nails,
Is every Hebrew's final share,
For beggar as for millionaire.

Though many an eye, behold, is wet;
Though all feel sorry, still they fret
Until the hearse starts off with me
Unto the Jewish cemet'ry.

But ere with fresh, damp earth all ends,
The last sad rites an old man tends;
He lifts the lid, and on his knees
Performs most curious cer'monies.

According to some ancient code,
Half-solemn and half-cruel mode,
With fragments of a broken cup
The eyes and mouth he covers up.

An earth-filled pillow 'neath the head,
A *taleth* * 'round the neck that's dead—
'Tis all according to the form
Of mystic, cabalistic norm;

* The sacred garb used by the orthodox as cover for head and shoulders during prayer.

As in the " Book of Life " 'tis writ—
Named " Book of Death " were better fit.
The ropes are placed, the box let down
Into the yawning grave, afrown.

Now men and shovels fill the tomb
With clay and maggots, night and gloom.
The grubs, I fear, will bring to naught
The resurrection we are taught.

And curious still, it seemed withal
My soul did hover o'er the pall.
It would abide on earth and stay
Until the corpse is laid away.

What next became of it, we'll trust
The future may reveal, and must,
Until its abode, bad or well,
Is fixed for paradise or hell.

But, after all, I'm glad to say
I died but in my fever. Ay,
These dreams and rhymes I gladly give
A little longer yet to live.

II.

Once more the fever made me wander;
　　I dreamed another, loftier sight:
My soul went to the life that's yonder,
　　Unto the Heavenly portals bright.
Yet there, with quick perceptive vision,
I noticed a most strange provision:

Some side-doors stood ajar; these portals
　　Were sally-points from whence approach
Long-bearded saints, once living mortals,
　　Who on my trembling soul encroach;
And every holy, hoary father
His neighbor crowds and tries to bother.

And when I made the exclamation:
　　"Who opes the main port unto me?"
You should have seen their consternation!
　　Each one contends that it was he,
If I would own their faith and power.
My answer made them start and cower:

"My faith is God—God, One, Eternal!"
　　And as the words I uttered, lo!
The Heavens opened; glory vernal—
　　No mortal comprehends it so—

Burst on my vivified conception,
A disenthralled soul's first reception.

A seraph came, and he conducted
 Me to the foot of God's High Throne.
By him I was forthwith instructed
 To kneel contrite, demure, and prone.
My judgment will, as all announce,
The Heavenly Father now pronounce.

A voice, awful, sublime, and stately,
 Spake forth these words—they sound
  like songs—
" My son! on earth thou suffered greatly.
 Thou wast a poet—all thy wrongs,
Though they were many, are forgiven;
Thou wast an author—enter Heaven!"

The angel my companion, nearing,
 A password whispered in my ears.
Through endless spaces we are steering—
 For wings had grown me unawares—
He led me thus to that collection
Inscribed: " The Poet's celestial section."

And here he left me as I entered.
 My goodness, what a sight was there!—

Soft, rosy light, in which was centered
   Capacious, but a crowded sphere.
Watch held one o'er the golden chapter—
   He seemed less poet than adapter.

"What hast thou written?" he demanded;
   "The *Febrile Frenzies!*" I replied.
"Read!" As the manuscript I handed
   It quickly at my head was shied.
He pointed at his stack of writing,
From which peered amours, crime, and fight-
     ing.

Were thus, then, all my ideals ending
   Of song immortal in spirit-lands?
As, searching, I my head was bending,
   In agony I wrung my hands!
Such trash in front! away back hidden
The masters, as if here unbidden.

Back to the throne of God I fluttered;
   Insane I stared and loudly cried:
"From Heaven banish me!"—then muttered,
   "Such a state Above as I descried.
I will be damned, in hell be roasted!"—
And then awoke, all wet, exhausted.

III.

I had my wish—it makes me cower—
   In Hades I was chained to brood
'Midst fire of the wildest power,
   With flames for garments, coals for food.

But still kept up rebellious pondering,
   Nor murmured, craven, with complaint;
Ne'er minding the caloric thundering,
   I bore all patient like a saint.

Had only not so noisy clamored
   Vile politicians, priests, and kings,
As they were scorched, and pinched, and
      hammered,
   Till with their howls *inferno* rings.

Ah! in the pool of fire eternal
   I noticed baking heads and hands.
To cinders changed all pomp external,
   Of bank and store, of seas and lands.

Oh, what a multitude of errors!
   What tigers, once disguised as lambs!
The pious, trusted, now in terrors;
   Aflame pretence, conceit, and shams.

But once a week, comes Friday even
    Here, too, reigns quiet, with fare of fish ;
And unto every sinner given
    Is then the granting of one wish.

Such lesson find in the Agadah,
    Of high Talmudic lore and fame ;
Yea, Sabbath-pudding,* a panada
    Comes to each suff'rer all the same.

Thus, red-hot, time was quickly flying.
    Of wings deprived, I had to roast.
My wrath calcined ; up went defying,
    In fire, all anger, pride, and boast.

When Friday came around, as usual
    My old friend seraph neared, and he
This time met not with a refusal
    In offering kindness unto me.

On earth I had left dearest kindred,
    Who must have learned that I was dead.
Oh! that I were no longer hinder'd
    To soothe their hearts, which must have
    bled.

---

* A Jewish dish well known by the name of " Kuchel.'

17

I would for once ask the permission
    Returning to yon mundane sphere;
Could such be done on the decision
    That I might wing myself from here.

Therefore I asked if he objected
    His pinions for a while to spare?
When instantly I too detected
    They grew upon my shoulders bare.

And quick I flew. It needed flying
    In my old German fatherland.
An angel would be law-defÿing,
    Were not a passport in his hand.

The Lord Himself they would imprison
    If He committed such offence.
So, turning upwards, I had risen
    And reached my old home-residence.

Hark! Midnight! every one is sleeping,
    Except my sorrowing people, who
Their pillows drench with bitter weeping,
    As only parents can and do.

Then slowly, softly I fanned slumber
   Upon their tear-sore, weary eyes.
Asleep their heart-aches, cruel, somber,
   To soothed consoling prayers rise.

Low-bending, their beloved features,
   I saw them, as in years ago.
Time, these adored and dear creatures
   Had kindly dealt with, spite their woe.

And now, in accents mild and tender,
   I whispered in their ears this strain:
" Dust all, we unto dust surrender,
   But by God's mercy meet again!"

Alas! I meanwhile thought in terror
   Of my confounded, cruel fate;
Of retribution, sin, and error.
   I rose again, for it grew late.

Poor seraph! I indeed feel sorry !
   Thou wilt not soon behold me more.
Without thy wings wilt have to worry
   Below in waiting, sad and sore.

Too far on high I rose; already
    Had sun and moon and comets scored.
When wide I 'woke, was calm and steady,
    And fully, God be thanked, restored!

And now that I can calmly ponder,
    May not our whole theology,
Our speculations on the Yonder,
    Such dreams of fever-frenzy be?

Lord! grant that when we wake hereafter,
    We fully be restored and well;
That we may mix our tears and laughter
    On our conceits of Heaven and Hell.

THE GERMAN VOLUNTEER, (1862.)

AMONG the maimed and slaughtered
In the field of fierce contest,
One of the dying soldiers—
    Shot through and through his breast—
Supported by his musket, he
    Convulsively did rise ;
Death rattled in his throat, and loud
    Yet tremulous he cries :

" I came across the ocean.
    At home I've been a slave.
I fought and die for liberty,
    And find a freeman's grave !
And if I had ten thousand lives
    I'd sacrifice them all
Ere I would see the Stars and Stripes
    A prey to traitors fall.

" Adieu, my wife and children
    Whom I abroad have left !
The God of babes and widows
    Protect you, now bereft !

And when hereafter peace returns,
  Columbia, ne'er forget
That many a sod beneath thy feet
  With foreign blood is wet.

" May Heaven guide this struggle,
  And keep the country free—
On earth the only refuge
  For life and liberty.
The Union one forever!—'gain
  On high the eagle soar!"
Thus shouts the German volunteer,
  And falls and is no more.

He saw not, knew not, 'round him
  Did silently gather then,
In deep and sad emotion,
  General, staff, and men.
They bore him on their muskets thence—
  Brave soldier's envied bier—
And buried him on the battle-field
  With many a sigh and tear.

A COURT SCENE.

(FROM AN ACTUAL OCCURRENCE.)

" MAY so it please your honor, my own case I would plead.
Assign me no attorney: I have no lawyers need.

And, gentlemen of the jury, my words may be uncouth,
I'll tell the truth!—I've sworn—and nothing ·but the truth:

I've killed the man—I own it; my weapon there you see;
And when you've heard my story you may do as you please with me.

Low creature they call me; I know it, my name is not of the best;
But still I am a woman, with feelings and rights of the rest.

My eyes and features reveal it, as true as
    God stamped Cain's ;
Indian blood and passion run hotly through
    my veins.

You know my husband left me—it was before
    I fell.
Abandoned, with hungry children, what others
    would do, you tell.

The night when this deed I committed, my
    youngest one lay sick
With burning, raging fever ; her breath came
    hot and thick.

There stands the doctor who told me with
    rest and nursing she'd live;
A mother, I trusted fondly in his restorative.

When outside, with boisterous clamor, crazy
    with drink and lust,
At midnight the man insisted that enter my
    house he must.

With tears I begged, I implored him not to
    disturb our peace,
But to the purpose only to make his rage
    increase.

He swore and raved; he clamored and
    threatened—then perfectly wild—
If the door I'd not quickly open he'd kill
    me and the child.

And then he fell in his fury to batter down
    the lock;
I cannot tell now was it with hammer or
    a rock.

I could not bear it longer; with none to help
    me near,
Frantic, grasped my weapon, and its report
    I hear.

What happened next I know not, but see, the
    man is dead;
It fits my pistol's barrel, from out his heart
    the lead.

If any of my sisters condemn my life of
    shame,
With Christian indignation a wicked woman
    blàme,

18

She throw the first stone upon me; but I do
  not refrain
To vow, the outrage repeated, that I would
  shoot again!

Such, gentlemen, is my story! My life is in
  your hand;
Bring in your verdict justly, as law and right
  demand.

But judge me as a mother; if I have acted
  wild—
Ah! I see tears here flowing—I did protect
  my child!

You will not leave the court-room—you have
  made up your mind?
" Not guilty," says the foreman; you all this
  verdict find?

I'm free? may go? God bless you! And
  now at once for home;
My heart yearns for my baby. Come, doctor,
  quickly come!

REMORSE.

T HE dreary night drags slowly by—
Will it be never morning?
Like mockery or scorning
Has hovered 'round, now far, now nigh,
The sleep I covet; but the eye
Is aching, painful burning.

There was a time I, too, enjoyed
· The balm of peaceful slumber—
Now all is dark and sombre;
For since I wilfully destroyed
My better self, by sin decoyed,
My woes are without number.

Look over there—on yonder wall,
Where night-lamp rays are crawling,
A sight which is appalling.
The words stick in my throat—I'd call—
O Heaven! is there no grace at all
For one who has been falling?

My feverish hands run through my hair.
That foul deed's apparition,
In sitting, stark position,

Involuntar'ly from my lair
It draws me; like insane I stare,
  And there behold perdition.

Curst and condemned!—I hear it coarse.
  My pulse grows thin and thinner.
  Ah! Satan has been winner.
Curst and condemned!—a voice speaks
    hoarse!
I scream in anguish and remorse:
  God pity a poor sinner!

NEVER, NEVER, NEVER!

A WANTON shot of a cruel hand
   Brought down the eagle from on high,
Crippling his wings. He flapped the sand,
  In vain endeavoring still to fly,
   His shrieks all agony, a strain
  Methought it was—the wild refrain:
    "My pure, blue sky, forever
    Our ties we must now sever,
For I can reach thee never—never—never!"

While furious gusts the waters lashed
  And rolled them back far out of reach,
One of the finny tribe was dashed,
  By storm, high on the rocky beach;
    Mute, eloquent the writhing pain
    Spoke dying, gasping the refrain:
      " My pure, green ocean, ever
      Our ties we must now sever,
For I can reach thee never—never—never!"

More sad than these, I saw a sight—
  A man, a human being, wrecked,
All battling in a deathly fight;
  For feign he'd rise, but e'er was checked
    By cruel fate. His heart and brain,
    All full of song, moaned the refrain:
      " My pure, high home, forever
      Our ties we must now sever,
For I can reach thee never—never—never!"

A CENTENNIAL POEM—1876. *

ONE hundred years only—one hundred
 years—
 The fathers of this nation,
'Midst hope and trembling, trust and fears,
 Signed Freedom's glorious proclamation.
In history's annals 'tis but like a day—
One hundred years only have passed away!

From world's end to world's end the mes-
 sage flew forth,
 To oppressed of all classes and people,
From East to West, from South to North,
 From city to hamlet, from palace to
 steeple.
Men welcomed it fervently near and far;
All hailed it—" Liberty's morning star ! "

Degraded pigmies of a giant race,
 How have you guarded the treasure?
Look at our realm, its shame and disgrace.
 It overflows the long-filled measure
Of misery, suff'ring, starvation, and
Crime stalking brazen through the land.

* At the time when this was written, as nearly everybody will remember,
the country was in a most deplorable condition.

Fanaticism and bigotry
   All nooks and corners are filling.
The dollar's almighty monopoly
   The people's blood is distilling.
Vile politicians govern the state,
And dramshops rule the Republic's fate.

Justice is blind, and deaf, and dumb;
   Law is but trick and contrivance;
Truth only is honored if bringing a crumb
   Of gain from lie and connivance;
And patriotism means now—the woe!—
Corruption in office, high and low.

There once was a time—the trembling lip
   Owns up the sad reflection—
To boast American citizenship
   Meant safety, honor, and protection;
While now the pettiest tyrant must
The "Stars and Stripes" trail in the dust.

Shall we, then, perish? Must we go down,
   Suicides cursed by damnation?
Despots' stigma, Liberty's frown,
   A byword—is there no salvation?
Devoid of hearts, of brains and hands,
Bearing the triflers' and cowards' brands?

Spirit of Washington, Franklin, and Clay,
   Spirit of martyr and hero,
Help us on High! and, if you may,
   Send us the man—be it Cato or Nero--
To raise this people from lethargy
And drive from the temple the Pharisee.

One hundred years hence, then—one hundred
     years—
   When thus is saved the nation,
'Midst hopes and trembling, trust and fears,
   Saved Freedom's glorious proclamation!
One hundred years hence—blessed be that
     day,   ·
From history never to pass away!

THE COLLECTOR'S WIFE.

A TRUE STORY.

"I'M dressed and waiting; supper is
 ready; the house is in trim and fix.
He told me he would be home at even—and
 now 'tis nearly six.
The cakes and cookies and dishes I've made
 he likes so well:
Man loves a woman better, if his taste she
 knows to tell.

"Hurrah! I hear his Bessy's neighing!
 Hark! he comes not alone!
I wonder who is his company—and—how
 long ere they'll be gone?
I rather had been without strangers; I know
 it is selfish and sin—
Not him? For the first time mistaken! They
 rap. Come in—come in!

"'What would ye with me? O Heaven!
 masked faces! My husband is gone,
 but then
You will not harm a helpless woman, if you
 are American men!
19

The money he has collected? the Govern-
    ment's revenue?
Kill me! but tell I'll never where 'tis hid-
    den; see if I do!

"'He placed it in my charge and keeping,
    leaving home—a trust'
Which while I live I'll not give over!   Try,
    if you dare and must!
Ye twist those ropes so tightly, they cut to
    the bone my hands.
I would not more have resisted without
    those cruel bands.'

"They're gone to search the house.   I'd
    scream, but, alas! no one is nigh.
They will not find the hidden treasure, let
    them till doomsday try!
Would that returned my husband and see
    me suffer here!
I'm shaking in my agony 'twixt pain, and
    hope, and fear.

"Hark! hark! they've found the coffer.   It
    staggers all belief.
Disgraced will be as a defaulter the man I
    love—a thief!

The Government will denounce him, all in
    his innocence.
Enough is money missing, convicting evi-
    dence.

"My limbs are free again; they bid me to
    give them supper quick.
An interposition of Heaven clearly, I see in
    this foolish trick:
These rogues tempt God their wickedness
    to punish; and, behold!
I am His humble instrument our honor to
    uphold.

"'Tis awful! they jest and they make merry
    so near the brink of death!
I see it work already in each short and
    heaving breath:
The poison is creeping surely and fatal
    through blood and brain.
They're dying and expiring! I'm safe and
    free again.

"Now quick I will unmask these villains,
    who thus their sex disgrace;
Perhaps that I can recognize one or the
    other's face.

Not one of all I'm knowing—here is the
    very last—
His mask off, too! I'll see him, since danger
    all is past.   .

" O horrible sight! O cruel vision! It can-
    not, cannot be—
My all, my loved one, O my husband! in
    this dread company.
Body and soul, and safety, love, happiness,
    all gone by ;
Housebreaker he and robber, and I, his mur-
    deress—I ! "

Frenzied, with hair dishevelled and flying,
    with countenance ghastly and pale,
She reaches, panting, a magistrate's office,
    and tells her fearful tale.
Her eyes are rolling wildly, her limbs and
    body shake ;
Madness follows her footsteps, and Death is
    in her wake.

Then as she staggers blind, and prostrate,
    expiring, falls to the floor,
Maniac-like, in the midst of people, she sud-
    denly rises once more,

With an effort wild and convulsive, until she
 is on her knees,
Broken exclaiming in prayer, as if inspired
 she sees:

"Have mercy, Lord, on us poor sinners, in
 love instead of right!
Oh! help us stray ones; make dark places
 with Thine forgiveness light.
My hus—band—!" And she mingles a tear
 with her last breath,
A loving, tender woman, beautiful unto
 death. •

THE RUSSIAN EXILE.

"O YE, who know what spell contains'
 the little word of home,
May ne'er ye feel the bitterness alone the
 world to roam,
Without a country, and without a friend or
 loving tie,
As now the Russian Exile must, a maiden-
 doomed as I:

"A stranger in a foreign land with language
 ne'er my own,
Like tree torn from its native soil wherein
 its youth had grown—
One who was reared in plenty's lap, midst
 luxury and ease;
Now thrown a pauper on the world, deprived of rest and peace.

"Deprived of all men value dear, naught,
 naught is left for me
Except the horror-striking claws of anguished
 memory.
That I but might, that I but could, events
 just past forget; -
That I could veil in blackest night the cruel
 fate I met;

"Could I forget how men like wolves and
 tigers ravenous grew,
And father, mother, kin and friends, in their
 wild frenzy, slew;
When axe and sickle ceased their work, how
 they, in ghoulish ire,
The lovèd corpses pitiless threw in the raging fire;

" How they compelled me, yet a child, to
 hush my moans and shrieks—
Look here, their nail-prints in my arm they
 dug in brutal freaks!
O God! O God! the memory it cleaves my
 heart in twain;
The recollections of my mind, they'll drive
 me yet insane.

" Behold, my hair is bleached in youth; it
 has grown silver-white.
No tongue will ever tell the tale, the horror
 of that night.
When unsexed women swore and raved, they
 swore and raved I must,
Right in their presence, fall a prey to carnal,
 brutal lust.

" I in my terror and despair shrieked loud
 for death or aid,
When strength came o'er me suddenly. Like
 tigress undismay'd
I fought. I snatched the axe from one next
 me; I smote her dead,
And, 'midst their consternation blank, into
 the night I fled.

"The forest jungle was more kind than aught
　　to me had been.
For weeks I dwelt in hidden cave, like
　　beasts live in their den;
I suffered hunger, parched with thirst—and
　　all this my own choice.
I dreaded nothing more than hear footfall of
　　man, or voice.

"I dared not sleep—I cannot sleep, for in
　　my haunted dreams
The whole dread tragedy will come o'er me
　　again, it seems.
At length philanthropists abroad, touched by
　　the cruel shame,
Succeeded in their efforts, they soon to our
　　rescue came.

"Thus I was saved and brought secure
　　across the ocean here.
Oh! thanks, kind friends; I see that you for
　　me will shed a tear.
My eyes with weeping have grown dry;
　　they feel so hot and sore—
My tears ran so incessantly. Henceforth I'll
　　weep no more.

"And why came all this misery on my de-
  voted head?
Why moulder in uncounted graves our poor
  unnumbered dead?
Why have the mobs, the craven mobs, in
  fury risen wild?
Why despots did permit to kill so mother
  and so child?

"O God of Israèl! for Thee — for Thee we
  suffered all.
For our religion we again, again as martyrs
  fall,
As martyrs in this age of light—so called—
  humane and kind,
While Russia tramps on human rights, fanati-
  cally blind!

"I have been taught from early youth not for
  revenge to pray,
'For vengeance is the Lord's '—is His, my
  pious teachers say.
But here upon my knees I lie and Sabaoth
  implore :
O Host of Justice! be Thou just unto Thine
  own once more!

20

"Nay, God have pity on their souls! No man
　　could bear the weight
That must be due to such as those with all
　　their dreadful freight
Of tears, of blood, of pangs and pain, of tor-
　　tured and of slain.
Have pity, God, upon their souls, nor let
　　me pray in vain!

"Thou hast permitted for some good our per-
　　secutors' wrath,
No doubt to lead Thy people 'gain upon
　　their mission's path.
Still, thanks to Thee! in my great need I
　　found Thee true, my God,
'Midst Israel in America — my Adonoy-
　　Echod!" *

＊ God the One.

THE ORPHAN ASYLUM IN VIENNA.

THE Emp'ror Josef of Austria—the one
of Hapsburg's clan
Who never had forgotten a prince is still a
man,
Who gained and valued people's love as his
most prized demesne—
Incognito did oft traverse his capital, old
" Wien." *

Relieved from flattering courtiers, from politicians free,
His eyes behold all stages of human misery ;'
Of suffering, hardship, wrong, and woe,
which undisguised appear.
Injustice then was oft redressed, and dried
up many a tear.

On such an expedition, as once the Emperor
went,
He met an aged sexton, who 'neath a burden
bent.

* The German name for Vienna.

Morose and solitary, the man moved slow
    and sore;
A little coffin of rough boards he on his
    shoulder bore.

His sympathy awakened, the Monarch gently
    says:
"What child is this you carry unto its rest-
    ing-place?
Is no one there to mourn the dead—no father,
    mother, kin?
No sorry heart, no tearful eye? It is a shame
    and sin!"

"Alas!" thus is made answer, with gruff,
    sardonic laugh,
"An orphan boy I bury; his parents' beggar-
    staff
Was all he e'er possessed on earth when
    found in fever's grasp
Upon the pavement of the street. 'Bread!'
    was his dying gasp!"

"Oh, may the Lord have mercy!" the deep-
    moved sovereign cried;
"A child in Christian country has of starva-
    tion died!"

He follows mourning to the grave, devoutly
  praying there,
As sorry as if the deceased one of his kindred were.

And when the little mound was erected on
  the ground,
His Majesty yet lingers, kneels down, like
  one spell-bound.
With upraised eyes and folded hands, the
  sunset on his brow,
Resembling saint or angel, he did make this
  solemn vow:

"Ne'er shall again my empire disgraced be
  and defiled;
For bread ne'er cry to Heaven a hungry
  orphan child
Within my realm — so help me God when
  comes my life's last hour!"
Most nobly was the promise kept, with bless-
  ings' fullest show'r.

The Emp'ror Josef of Austria had many a
  monument built;
His noble deeds are written in marble and
  in gilt;

Yet long when these have perished lives his
    mem'ry, graced and green,
As founder of the "Orphan Home" which
    bears his name in "Wien."

THE ORIGIN OF THE DIAMOND.*

LISTEN to the curious story
    How the Diamond in its glory
Grew amidst the giant blocks
In the strata of the rocks;
How the precious stone was wrought
From a spark of light and thought;
Love-light shining on our earth.
In a tear the gem had birth.
Thought, to light and love obedient,
Its most pure and prized ingredient.

As from presence of the Lord
Satan and his rebel horde,
By ambition wild and fell,
Hurled were into deepest hell—

* Oriental Legends, written after the others were in print.

Doomed to fire, fear, and pain,
Without sunshine, light, or rain—
Mercy, the bright angel, crept
To the throne of God and wept
A hot tear, in deep prostration,
E'en for Hades' last salvation.

And this drop, so tells the story,
Grew a jewel in its glory,
Falling 'midst the giant blocks
In the strata of the rocks.
As an emblem it was wrought,
Sparkling light, and love, and thought.
Crystallized proclaims the tear,
Final quenching fire and fear!
Heaven's promise, Mercy's token,
Are, like diamonds, never broken.

URIEL DA COSTA.

[A Jewish refugee from Portugal, where he and his family had been forced
into Catholicism.　On arriving in Amsterdam he rejoined Judaism.　Soon,
however, by his free-thought, he came in conflict with the Rabbins, and had to
do public penance. Mortified by this humiliation, he killed himself, A.D. 1644.]

CURSED by the holy Synagogue,
　　Is he a sinner, knave, or rogue?

With folded hands, but knitted brow,
Before the Rabbins he does bow;

A culprit, made to bend his knee
In shame and penance.　Who is he?

A man who, in the dark of night,
Has seen the dawning of the light.

By glorious visions all inspired,
The house of prejudice he fired.

Not asking how it burn and scorch,
He lit and waved the flaming torch,

And narrow-mindedness felt weak.
Oh! how the hypocrites did shriek.

And how fanatics clamored wild,
"'Sanctum Sanctorum' is defiled!"

Thus loud goes forth their hue and cry!
Will might prevail, and tyranny?

The grand "Sanhedrin" does decree:
"Renounce thy false philosophy!

"A heretic thou art, defamed;
The *Cherem godoul* * we proclaimed!"

Who in that malediction stays
Were better dead those cruel days,

When ignorance takes quick in hand
What superstition does command;

Of all the stiff-necked, stubborn crew,
The worst is a fanatic Jew.

The people and their priests combine;
They have him at the sacred shrine.

All tóo unequal is the fight—
They bid him say that wrong is right!

And though his heart and soul be rent,
They made him own it: "I repent!"

Repent he said, the book records;
He spoke the bitter, hateful words.

Upon his neck they placed their feet,
His humiliation to complete.

---

* The anathema of the Rabbins in former times when they had ecclesiastical jurisdiction.

Nor Moses nor the Prophets cite
Such Catholic-inquisition rite.

But Israelites in Holland try
What Spanish monks but justify;

Which proves: no folly is so great
Blind zealots will not imitate.

But while at times men have been hushed,
The Truth proclaimed, was never crushed!

Such seed once sown will grow along
For harvest sure, almighty strong!

The little souls their work have done;
They thought extinguished was the sun,

Since they had shut their sleepy eyes
And grinned so mighty and so wise.

But though ere this men had been hushed,
God's truth proclaimed, is never crushed!

Thus while their victim's heart ached sore,
Da Costa's name lives evermore.

A DOCTOR'S PANEGYRIC

BEFORE THE ANNUAL MEDICO SOCIETY.

L ADIES and Sirs! Most welcome here,
    dear friends ;
And while I'd make for my poor words and
    rhymes amends,
Pray give ye close attention for the task
    assigned,
To eulogize our calling—one most high and
    kind,
        The noblest of all missions:
        Profession of Physicians.

Not that I would attempt to slur or under-
    rate
Other crafts and arts. Society and state,
Mankind for its development and fullest
    strength
Requires them, too, in fullest width, and
    height, and length.
        Bless all that break a fetter
        Or make us nobler, better !

But thrice blest certainly should be the
　　earnest man,
Devoting all his life, whate'er he is and can,
To alleviate the pangs and suff'ring of our
　　kind—
The sick, the weak, the halt, the lame and
　　blind,
　　　　The sore in heart and feeling—
　　　　By the great art of healing.

There is no season, hot or cold, the doctor
　　may
Look for his ease or comfort.　In stormiest
　　night or day
He must be ready at a patient's slightest
　　call.
Hungry, thirsty, though the eyes with sleep
　　may fall,
　　　　None of all these are heeded,
　　　　He's at his post when needed.

For wisdom to High Heaven he directs his
　　eye.
He watches close and reads the changes of
　　the sky.

Into the bowels of the earth · he arduous
dives
For treasures there concealed which will
save human lives.
    All nature he'll explore,
    Health failing to restore.

The min'rals turn to medicines at his · be-
hest.
The vegetable realm gives balm at his re-
quest.
The animal kingdom, too, waits his command
To turn restorative at his benignant hand.
    , E'en poison's deathly ranges
    Into health-power he changes.

Have ever you been vouchsafed, closely to
behold
The anxious looks of all the household,
young and old,
When o'er the baby-suff'rer their kind doctor bends and bides?
He counts the pulse; all breathless wait till
he decides:
    Is pet · to live? God save her!
    Or go to Him who gave her?

Have e'er you stood close by when mother,
 seeming low,
In fever's grasp, her waning breath comes
 hot and slow;
When husband, sons, and daughters silent,
 tearful pray
Her to be safe, and hear at last the doctor
 say,
  "Thank Heaven, I fear no longer—
  The crisis left her stronger"?

And oh! the grief and sorrow when, in spite
 of skill
And all that can be done by science and
 best of will,
At last grim Death will claim the suff'rer as
 his own,
Amidst the woe, the tears, the sobs, heart-
 rending groan,
  Dumbfounded, mute appealing—
  Ay, doctors too have feeling!

Many an hour and many a day is thus made
 sad
In vigils from the cradle to the grave. And
 add

That this oft happens 'midst the ranks of
veriest poor—
An evil for which there seems neither help
nor cure—
>> Take all in all, and can we
>> The good profession envy?

Still, our reward is: duty well and true per-
formed;
Grief stilled that in some bosom wildly raged
and stormed;
Tears dried which would in anguish all unbidden flow;
And pallid cheeks with health and color
made to glow.
>> Unselfish satisfaction,
>> Man's best of thought and action!

To strengthen such great purpose, foster such
high ends,
Assemble, here in council yearly, all true
friends.
Once more, then, welcome! Let us prove by
work combined
To elevate our calling—one most high and kind,
>> The noblest of all missions:
>> Profession of Physicians.

AN APPEAL TO AMERICA

AGAINST SECTARIAN AGITATIONS.

THOU, too, great, glorious, free-born
      dame,
Art urged to black thy unstained name,
With persecution's foulest shame.

Thou, too, upon thy favored soil,
Art called upon to join the spoil
For which barbarians toiled and toil.

The Nineteenth Century looks on
With all it has for mankind done,
And trembles for thy victories won.

Thy heroes dead, in reverenced graves
O'er which immortal triumph waves,
Fanaticism taunts and braves.

The grandest of prerogative,
Thy great palladium, conceive
Torn, desecrated, positive,

Except thou stay the upraised hand
Which in this time and in this land
Would curse thy brow with Cain's vile brand;

Except thy foot, O giantess!
Comes down in ire, stern for redress,
As raise thy arms in tenderness;

Except thou bid each creed and church:
" Here is no room where Hatred's torch
For bloody strife and tears may search;

" But in this realm of wide expanse
Reigns Liberty's deliverance
In panoply of Tolerance!"

23

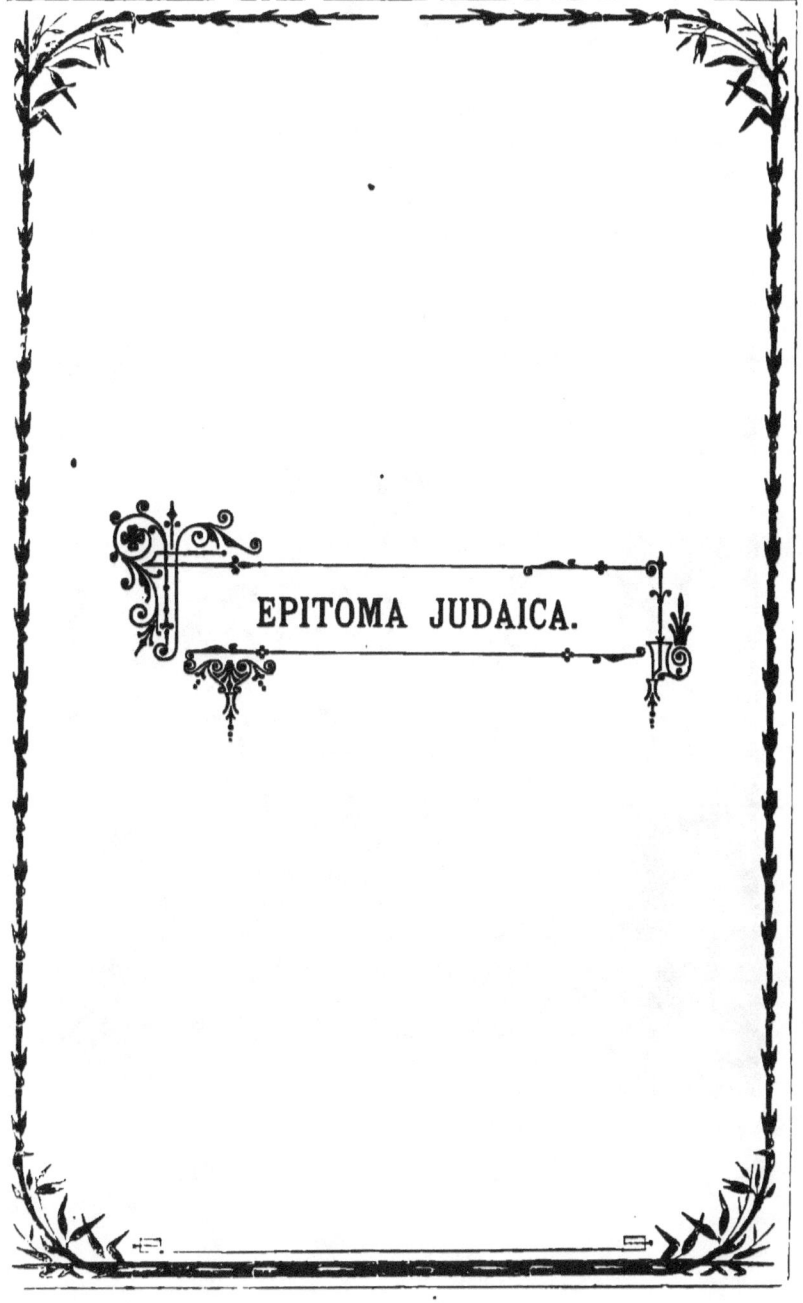

EPITOMA JUDAICA.

"Behold in marble chiselled the ideal!"—PART III., p. 197.

EZEKIEL'S STATUE OF RELIGIOUS LIBERTY.

Epitoma Judaica.

DEDICATORY ADDRESS

AT THE ERECTION IN PHILADELPHIA, 1876, *OF*
EZEKIEL'S STATUE : RELIGIOUS LIBERTY.

PART FIRST.

THE themes immortal sung by bards
    have been
Of glorious nations and heroic men;
And tears and smiles a verse has often
    stirred,
A tale of fate which conquered, loved, or
    erred.
For in all times, no matter where and when,
Like unto birds of mountain, dell, and glen,
Man sings of goal attained and hope deferred.
Thus came these rhymes; if lacking beauty's
    grace,
Indulge the nosegay, though in broken vase.

There lives a people in whose very name
Is centred human glory and their shame—

A people whose proud records plainly tell
How earth can be made paradise or hell.
This nation, who has wrought its own high
    fame,
Bright from the furnace of its trials came;
May I forget my right hand, Israel,
If I forget thee—thee to whom belongs
Whate'er is worthy in these humble songs!

'Tis near four thousand years when there
    went forth
The patriarch who, chosen for his worth,
Was bid, as told in the Old Testament,
Upon his mission of world-wide extent
To go and " bless all nations of the earth,"
By making declarations of the birth
Of Heaven's will, revealed most eloquent
In this one sentence: " Adonai Echod!" *
Which means: There is but One, one only
    God.

As chaos vanished at the grand behest,
" Let there be light!"—light, Heaven's gift
    the best!—
So was the darkness in the moral world
Into the abyss of dread destruction hurl'd.

            * God is but One.

For this one revelation forms the crest
Of Abram's unique, precious, grand bequest.
From thence was Israel's banner wide un-
    furl'd—
One God! the watchword in its simple
    phrase;
One God! the mission for all future days.

The slave in Egypt, who beneath his chains
And grievous burdens groaned and bore his
    pains,
Inflicted by the heartless master's whip—
The cruel hands that smote him thigh and
    hip—
While he whate'er is brutal still sustains,
In spite of all, the strongest trust maintains.
His eyes dilate, his convulsed musc'lar grip
The task performs, with breath of life near
    gone,
Great in despair, believes: "God is but
    One!"

And Moses came and saved his shackled
    race.
The freedmen stand on awe-topped "Sinai's"
    base,

And there, from out of thunder, clouds, and
    flame,
Eternal truth, the laws of mankind came.
"I am thy God!" Be free! have love and
    grace.
Heaven folding Earth, her mate, in fond em-
    brace,
"Amen!" did loud the universe proclaim.
Our globe turned into one great Synagogue,
And benediction was—the decalogue.

"I am thy God—One God!" This is the
    key
To all found subsequent in history.
Complex as proves the lock of life, 'twill fit
To ope the treasure stored in holy writ.
In secular annals naught is mystery—
Fiat to doubt! quietus to sophistry!
Science and reason shall in judgment sit,
Like mathematics, solving this One-say,
The darkness of the past, the light to-day.

Israel, dwelling in fair Palestine,
Built a temple and its holy shrine,
Slowly and gradually, but firm stepped on,
Developing the truth of "God the One";

Oft staggering, erring, clouding the Divine,
Sure paying for its frequent sins the fine.
But in transgressing, too, the work was done,
For nothing clogs the wheel of fixed intents:
E'en folly is one of God's instruments!

A chosen people, by divine decree
Recipients they and guardians were to be
Of an eternal law—a principle—a truth !
Yet they were men in weakness, faults, for-
    sooth,
And oft to idols turned and bent the knee—
And with our vast experience so do we.
Nor to become exclusive or uncouth
Were they elected. Models they should shine
In all that's noble, virtuous, good, and fine.

When, by the rule of evolution true,
Some other nations reached the standard, too,
At which they should and ought partake of
    right,
The knowledge of the truth, the bliss of light,
'Twas then the holy land too narrow grew :
The Temple fell ; the Hebrew bade adieu
To home and sacred shrine, in tears and
    fright.

24

As every birth is wrapt in pangs and fear,
So men do enter on each new career.

Well may the wand'rer sorrow when he leaves
His home and country; when he pines and
    grieves
From all that is deemed dear and loved to
    part.
Well may the pilgrim mourn with trembling
    heart,
But, knowing what he loses, not conceives
The goal before him; and the dream he
    weaves
Is to return e'en ere he makes a start.
Hebrew, go forth again! God's frowns and
    smiles
Extend His will beyond a few square miles!

Twice lay Jerusalem in ashes. Rome
Engraved in human blood the epitome
Of her destructive instincts. Captive, slave,
Israel as a nation found its grave
Among the seven hills; beneath the dome
It built the Coliseum. Stone and loam
Were merciful compared to Titus brave.

But "Adonai Echod" remained their code,
In history the grandest episode.   .

PART SECOND.

There is no standstill in events, but thought
    will often pause,
Reflecting on the logic stern of consequence
    and cause.
Right here some heroes of this world might
.   well a lesson learn—
Those who oppressed would freedom and their
    independence earn;
Invincible God's people were while Union
    there presided:
The first-best conqueror laid them low when
    they became divided.

Events went on, and very soon the clash of
    nations came;
Fierce cohorts fell upon cohorts; the world
    shook in her frame.
The Hun against the Roman struck, the Nor-
    man 'gainst the Hun;
The Teuton, Anglo-Saxon, all in battle's circle
    spun.

From one end of the continent of Europe to
    the other,
Each tribe and clan seemed bent upon his
    neighbor's life to smother.

And when the clash of armor ceased, Rome
    was no more, nor Greece;
New rulers occupied the thrones, new thoughts
    came with the peace.
An humble child of Nazareth, of Jewish
    parents born,
A martyr on the crucifix, wreathed with a
    crown of thorn—
He preached the law, he taught reform, to
    worship the Creator;
He died the death at Roman hands, as died
    with them the traitor.

Meek, simple, loving words his were, full of
    God's spirit each,
In different terms but self-same sense as Law
    and Prophets teach.
His followers were few at first, but soon in
    numbers swelled,
And then increased to multitudes that were
    unparalleled.

But as they grew, his thoughts, his words,
    his labors were deserted ;
They changed the teacher to a God: his
    mission was perverted.

At least so thought the Jews ; and so they
    think this very day.
One God for them was well enough in whom
    to trust, to pray.
One only God—no Trinity—is what their
    Scriptures teach ;
Let whosoever dare this faith, yet unim-
    peached, impeach.
And since they would not join the crowd as
    followers and suitors,
They were accused and soon decried the
    Saviour's persecutors.

The new creed met vicissitudes and suffered
    martyrdom,
From under which a cause grows strong and
    never does succumb.
Had men but learned the lesson then, what
    tolerance should be—
"Do unto others as ye would that others
    do to ye!"

But once their trials changed to power, in
    hamlet, town, and city
They placed their feet upon the necks of
    others without pity.

What then was done and there was done it
    harrows heart and soul,
In Christ's name and religion's name all o'er,
    from pole to pole.
The curse again went forth from Rome,
    launched out the blasting cue:
"Move on! move on! forever on! proscribed
    and outcast Jew.
Like Cain, find never rest, nor peace, nor
    place to live, nor shelter.
Move on! Who finds thee has permit in
    Hebrew blood to welter."

"Move on!" shrieked Italy, "Move on!"
    in her intensest strain.
"Move on!" Spain echoed shrill, "Move
    on!" O cruel, cruel Spain!
France, Germany, and Britain cried, and
    every petty prince:
"Move on, Jew, move! no matter how you
    suffer, cry, and wince."

Such horror, devilish outrage fill that pe-
   riod's blood-stained pages,
Such misery, barbarity—well are they called
   "Dark Ages!"

Behold this tableau: On his knees, the eyes
   raised up on high,
As if imploring Heaven and man against such
   tyranny;
Each feature speaks of agony—the hands
   clutched in his hair;
Wife, children, crouching by his side, a picture of despair.
The Jew moves on, forever on, and hither,
   thither wanders,
Still trusting "Adonai Echod!"—a faith he
   never slanders.

Like hunted game the Israelite seeks refuge
   in the caves;
He loses all—no matter, if the scroll of law
   he saves.
There is no war but that recoils upon his
   head a scourge,
No peace is made but brings him near anni-
   hilation's verge.

Well might he sing in David's words, with
    tones that sadly quiver:
"How long, O Lord, before Thou wilt Thy
    stricken ones deliver?"

Somehow submissively they lived and patient-
    ly endured.
They prayed, they learned, they worked, they
    hoped, but ne'er their creed abjured.
No retaliating hand they raised through cen-
    turies of woe—
Who ever knew a Jew to take revenge upon
    his foe?
To "Adonai Echod" belongs the judgment!
    so no wonder
Fanatics, priestcraft, tyranny, not Israel,
    went under.

PART THIRD.

The nightmare-dream, the terror, all is o'er;
Changed are the passions which had ruled
    of yore;
The storms that raked humanity are past;
From out of darkness light breaks forth at
    last.

Free breathes the lover of his race once
  more;
Intolerance is smitten root and core.
The ship of state has "Progress" for her
  mast;
A flag she flings out at her topmost staff,
Won by the press, and steam, and telegraph.

Miraculously these noble powers have wrought;
All that's humane is in close contact brought.
Hate, prejudice, the rule of sword and fist,
No more can in our century exist.
Well are the battles of enlight'ment fought;
The victory belonged to God and human
  thought!
Chief adjutant has been the scientist—
Who would have prophesied it? Rome and
  Spain
In this great revolution led the main!

For while their savage inquisitions yet
The deadly instruments of torture whet
'Neath which their life-blood heretics to spurt,
The victims to convince thus and convert—
Columbus brave his ships and sailors met,
And westward ho! his sails of empire set.

25

A world he found, compared to which inert
The old one should become—America, thee!
Creation's pearl! God's home for liberty!

Nor came it all at once! 'Tis true, they say:
"The laws of Heaven slowly work their way!"
The ocean, when upheaved, shows long his
    might,
And morning dawns but gradually from night.
It would take volumes, not a roundelay,
To record the slow gait of reason's sway—
How people learned to see the wrong from
    right,
How sages tackled folly, crime, and fault,
How men of iron nerves dared to revolt.

All hail to France! The foremost torch she
    lit;
Headlong she dared the strongest blow to
    hit
By which the hold of tyranny was rent
From all of Europe. The whole continent
With trembling saw the bold, unswerving grit,
And slow but surely imitated it,
Decreeing, 'midst the despot's fear and awe,
Mankind's equality before the law!

All hail to Germany, too, the fatherland!—
Though now once more she hurls the fire-
    brand
Against her children. She will bewail ere
    long
Her latest crime, her monstrous, insane
    wrong.
Still shall her sons erect and proud yet stand.
From out this crisis grows a free-born band
Of brothers, singing the sublimest song.
A free republic will all creeds combine:
" Eine feste Burg "* and " Wacht am Rhein!" †

All hail, Britannia, free and noble isle!
We have forgot our wrongs beneath thy
    smile.
Since " Magna Charta" came to rule and
    bless,
Like lightning flew oppression and distress.
Her sentiments are truth, her law no guile;
She knows but citizens—one vast, great pile,
Secure beneath her reign. In tenderness
God bless her! and clear that last stern
    frown!—
May Ireland, too, be jewel to her crown!

* Rock of Ages. † Guard of the Rhine.

All hail, too, Italy! All hail, too, Spain!
Though ye have caused our tears to flow
    like rain,
And slow e'en now to follow in the wake
Of roads which more enlightened people
    take.
Ye may, with Russia and few others, strain
Against the spirit of the time. 'Tis vain!
Beware, lest Heaven, outraged, crush and
    shake
You, dome and pit, and lay you in the dust!
For in our days men will be free, and must!

Yes, hail, accursed Russia! Sure as fate
Full retribution will come soon or late,
For every drop of blood, for every tear,
For every anguish, every cry of fear
From orphans and from widows sent   on
    High;
For murder, outrage, violence, and, fie!
Child-slaying—in our days, fresh in our ear—
As infamous these deeds are in our time,
Will sevenfold seven Russia wail the crime.

While "Glory! Hallelujah!" loud and long,
Unto America shall be the song:

The Centenarian Republic live!
Cheers upon cheers united let us give!
Youngest of the nations! to thee belong
The honors that thy founders skyward flung,
The banner of our great prerogative,
The declaration of our liberty:
.ALL MEN ARE *INDEPENDENT!* EQUAL!!
FREE!!!

In this rich panoply of manhood decked,
The Jew again stands forth, restored, erect.
He may untrammelled worship God, the
    Great,
With others, as their consciences dictate.
Men, citizens, regardless creed or sect,
May loyal live, believe as they elect,
Without reproach to fellow-men or hate.
Our Hebrew people act as prototypes;
Hew down the arm raised 'gainst the Stars
    and Stripes!

Behold in marble chiselled the ideal
Of all we suffered, passed, and loved, and
    feel:
" Religious Liberty!" with eyes on high,
Eagle and snake " Intolerance crushed" imply.

The Innocent makes by her side appeal
That light may future, better days reveal.
And if you ask us for the reason why,
Then thus be told: Fast comes the reign of
    God
When mankind owns it—ADONAI ECHOD!

THE END.